THE DOOR IN THE TREE

The four books of THE MAGICIAN'S HOUSE cover an eventful year in the lives of the Constant children; William, Mary and Alice. Their parents, both doctors, are away, working at a hospital in Africa and consequently the school holidays are being spent with Uncle Jack and Phoebe at Golden House, in The Golden Valley, an area of wild country on the Welsh borders.

In the first book the children discovered the Steps up the Chimney and the secret room at the top of the tower. Here they met Stephen Tyler, an Elizabethan alchemist and magician, who has discovered the secret of time travelling. Under his instruction they themselves experienced some of the magic that he has mastered. They entered into the bodies and minds of the Magician's friends; Spot, the Dog, Cinnabar, the Fox, and Jasper, the Owl; they learnt a little about alchemy and they started on the mysterious great task that the Magician has set them. By their own courage they thwarted the endeavours of Morden, the Magician's evil assistant (still locked in his own time in the 16th century, but with the ability to reach out with his influence into the children's modern day world) and, with their help, Jack and Phoebe's baby, Stephanie, was safely born.

Now, in the second book, it is spring, and the children have returned for the Easter holidays. The world of nature is awakening for another year and they are about to enter once more into the magic and to continue their

The Magician's House Quartet
The Steps up the Chimney
The Door in the Tree
The Tunnel Behind the Waterfall
The Bridge in the Clouds

Two double videos of the highly acclaimed BBC TV
series 'The Magician's House' are available from High
Street stores or by calling Acorn Video on
020 7801 9668. Each video contains an entire series.
For more details check out the Acorn Video
website www.acornmedia.com

THE DOOR IN THE TREE

Being the Second Book of The Magician's House

William Corlett

RED FOX

For Alice

A Red Fox Book

Published by Random House Children's Books
20 Vauxhall Bridge Road, London SW1V 2SA

A division of The Random House Group Ltd
London Melbourne Sydney Auckland
Johannesburg and agencies throughout the world

First published in Great Britain in 1991 by
The Bodley Head Children's Books

Red Fox edition 1992
This Red Fox edition 1999

5 7 9 10 8 6

Printed and bound in Great Britain by
Cox & Wyman Ltd, Reading, Berkshire

THE RANDOM HOUSE GROUP Limited Reg. No. 954009

Papers used by The Random House Group Limited
are natural, recyclable products made from wood grown in
sustainable forests. The manufacturing processes conform to
the environmental regulations of the country of origin.

ISBN 0 09 940767 1

www.randomhouse.co.uk

Contents

THE DOOR IN THE TREE

1
Hide and Seek

Alice ran as fast as she could up the hill, away from the stump where Mary was counting aloud, with her hands covering her eyes. William, meanwhile, scrambled into the undergrowth along the side of the forest track and, at a distance from him, a flash of white marked where Spot was bounding away from the block, his tail wagging as he tried not to bark with excitement.

It was a bright spring day with a breeze blowing. It shook the branches of the trees and made them sway and move above Alice's head, clattering and swishing. Reaching the cover of a clump of gorse bushes, she paused, gasping for breath, and looked around her. The first green buds had opened along the hedgerows and primroses, wild daffodils and violets pushed up through the moss and dead leaves that covered the bank on which she crouched.

Across the valley, through a gap in the forest, she could just see the top of the dovecote in the kitchen garden and beyond it, the roof and chimneys of Golden House. The familiarity of the view made her feel at home. Although this was only her second visit to the place, she already knew the lie of the land. There was something comforting about

1

recognizing landmarks, she thought. It meant that you couldn't get lost. William was so pompous about having the compass, but really all you needed was to use your eyes.

Down below, Mary's voice rose in volume as she neared 'a hundred'. Alice pulled back behind the gorse bushes and crouched lower, waiting, with her heart pounding. She hadn't actually wanted to play hide and seek, in fact she thought it a complete waste of time, but now that they'd started, she couldn't help getting caught up in the game.

It was the first day of the Easter holidays, or rather, it was the first day of their visit to Golden House. All three children had spent Easter weekend with friends in London and then come on by train, via Bristol, the day before.

Phoebe had been waiting for them at the station and they'd driven back through the early evening haze, reaching the house as the last light finally drained from the sky and darkness settled over the valley.

Jack had been in the kitchen washing his hands at the sink when they'd come in and Spot had appeared from nowhere, rushing towards them, barking and licking and jumping with such enthusiasm that he'd knocked Alice off her feet and then landed on top of her, covering her face with his wet tongue while she happily screamed and protested.

Stephanie, who'd been sleeping in her cot, had been woken by all this commotion and joined in with a strong bellowing so that the whole house, which a moment before had been silent, echoed and reverberated with noise.

'Oh, Lord!' Jack had yelled, covering his ears

and laughing. 'You're back! I'd forgotten how noisy you brats can be!' and he'd pushed Spot off Alice and yanked her up on to her feet and given her a hug.

Later he'd gone with them up to their rooms at the top of the spiral staircase above the great hall and he'd sat on Mary's bed and talked while they unpacked. He was full of all the work he'd been doing on the house and all the surprises he'd found; 'The cellars and the attics and bits of old junk and goodness knows what else', he'd told them excitedly. But they hadn't really been listening to him. They'd wanted to be on their own, to savour the pleasure of being back. They hadn't even wanted to share the moment between themselves. They'd each wished that they were entirely alone so that they could hug themselves and run to the window and look out or lie on the bed and stare up at the steeply pitched ceilings of their rooms, with the dark wooden beams and cobwebs and white, flaking plasterwork.

Then Phoebe had called them down and they'd had supper round the kitchen table and everyone had started to talk at the same time about what had been happening to them since they were last together. They'd eaten thick bean soup, followed by vegetable stew and jacket potatoes stuffed with cheese. After that there was a treacle tart for dessert and Alice had had a second helping and thought for a moment that she was going to burst, but the others ignored her alarm and so she'd eaten an apple as well. Finally all the excitement of the day and the travelling had got the better of them and the children had crawled back up the stairs to their rooms once more and were tucked up in bed and fast asleep before the clock in the hall chimed nine.

Now, as Alice crouched in hiding, she thought it had been a bit of a disappointment, really. All through the spring term she'd dreamed of Golden House and of the magic and particularly of Spot. There had been no one she could share the memories with. Mary was in senior school now and she never saw her, William was away in Yorkshire, and of course, they'd made a Solemn Vow on the last day of the Christmas holiday not to speak about anything that had happened to them while they were at Golden House to anyone but each other.

So the term had come to an end but then, when they were staying with their friends in London, they'd had no chance to talk at all. She'd expected the subject at least to be mentioned when they were on the train yesterday, but the other two had read books and wouldn't be drawn into any conversation about their previous visit to Uncle Jack's house. In fact when Alice had mentioned the Magician, Mary had kicked her on the shin under the table and William had hissed at her to shut up, because people might be listening.

So Alice had sat with her hands under her thighs and swung her legs and hummed a tuneless little song and stared glumly out of the window until they reached Bristol.

While they'd waited for their connection she'd been too busy eating sausages in the station buffet for any conversation. The stockpiling of the sausages was a sensible precaution against Phoebe's vegetarian cooking and she'd planned it well in advance. She thought it was probably the sort of preparation a camel would undertake before making a long journey across the desert – only she hadn't got a hump and half way through the third jumbo sausage she had felt a bit sick and left the rest of it on the paper plate.

The little train had been crowded with people so they hadn't even managed to sit together. Alice had got a window seat and stared out at the passing scene. The sausages were stuck like a lump in her stomach and the central heating in the carriage was turned up high. She'd felt hot and a bit depressed. She'd been looking forward to it all so much, but William and Mary seemed to have forgotten everything, which was typical of them and exceedingly boring.

Phoebe had been waiting for them at Druce Coven Halt and once they were in the Land-Rover there had been again no possibility of private conversation. Finally, when they'd reached the house, they'd been with Uncle Jack the whole time until they went up to their rooms. Then Mary did at one point say, almost grudgingly Alice thought, that they should have a conference after supper; but when that time came, they couldn't any of them keep their eyes open and were almost asleep before they'd each staggered into their beds. Consequently it wasn't until the following morning that they had had any time to themselves.

Soon after breakfast Mary had suggested going out to explore the forest.

'Don't go too far,' Jack had warned them. 'The paths are pretty obvious, but it can get a bit confusing after a while.'

'We won't get lost,' William had assured him.

'I've been doing orienteering at school. Have you got a large scale map, Uncle Jack?'

But Jack had shaken his head and said he'd been meaning to get one, but hadn't so far got round to it. There was an ordinary map but it wasn't a big enough scale to be useful in the forest. 'You need one that marks the footpaths and tracks,' he told them.

Phoebe said she'd try to get one when she went into town, later in the morning.

'A map really is needed,' William had said, 'if we're going to explore properly. With a map and a compass you can never get lost.'

Alice had sighed at this and bit back a catty remark. William was at his most pompous and she loathed him when he got into one of those moods, but she'd thought it best not to have a row with him straight away; not so soon after they'd arrived.

Phoebe had suggested they might like to go with her when she went shopping.

'The town's quite nice really. There's a castle of sorts. Well, it's more of a tower really. Built by the English to suppress the Welsh. Or maybe it was built by the Welsh to threaten the English. My history is hopeless.'

Mary perked up at this, because history was her favourite subject. But this had been the final straw for Alice.

'If Mary's going to start giving a history lesson,' she'd announced, unable to contain her irritation a moment longer, 'I'm definitely going out,' and she'd run to the back door to put on her shoes.

William had agreed with Alice – once Mary

started on history it could last for hours – but he didn't say so. Instead he followed her to the door.

'If you get us a map, Phoebe,' he'd said, 'it'd be really good. You can't orienteer properly without one.'

But he took his compass anyway and, when they'd all put on shoes, he'd set off in the lead in a rather bossy way, which infuriated Alice even more and made Mary lag behind as though she was 'not being with them' in a rather pointed way.

They'd gone through the kitchen garden, passing the dovecote, and out through a gate in the back wall, which Jack had told them led to where the forest track skirted the back of the estate. Once there, William had paused, deciding which direction to take, and Alice had caught him up, followed shortly after by Mary.

'I don't believe you two,' Alice had said, trying not to sound disappointed and sounding cross instead.

'Now what's the matter?' William had asked, concentrating on the compass.

'William!' Alice had exploded, shaking with exasperation. 'Surely you haven't forgotten?'

But William had only stared more closely at the compass and Mary had crossed away from them to lean against a fence, with her back to them both.

'I've waited all term for this . . . ' Alice started again, but now she'd been interrupted by the sound of Spot barking at a distance, and a moment later he appeared from the direction of the kitchen garden, tail wagging.

'Oh, Spot,' Alice had cried, flinging her arms round the dog's neck. 'You remember, don't you?

You remember how the Magician made it possible for me to be in you and see through your eyes and smell through your nose? You remember how we raced together across the snow. . . . Please tell me you do, Spot. You know you can. You can talk in my head, can't you? That's what happened. We did, didn't we? Please say we did . . . '

But Spot had only gazed up at her with pleading eyes and had put his head on one side as though he was trying desperately to understand her words.

This had been more than Alice could bear. If Spot didn't remember, then no one would. That meant no one in the world remembered . . . except her.

'What is going on?' she'd said to herself and she'd frowned and sat on her haunches and scratched her cheek, always a sign that she was thinking deeply.

But William had turned slowly and looked at her.

'Of course I remember,' he'd said in a low doubting voice, then he'd quickly looked away again, concentrating once more on his compass.

'You do?' Alice had cried out, relieved. 'I thought I was going crazy. Oh, Will – why won't you talk about it then?'

'I've thought a lot about it. But . . . it couldn't have happened,' William had said quietly. 'I mean . . . it isn't possible.'

'It did, though,' Mary then joined in. 'Somehow it did.'

'But, of course it did!' Alice had exclaimed. 'What's wrong with you both? Why are you behav-

8

ing so strangely?' And she knelt on the ground, looking up at them with desperate eyes.

'I'm not,' William had replied. 'I can't explain. It's just . . . well, it isn't possible – magic, I mean. So . . . if it isn't possible . . . it didn't happen.'

'But we all know it did happen – all of it,' Alice could have hit him, she felt he was being so stupid. 'What will you say if it happens now? That you're dreaming it? I'd like to know how we could all three of us have had the same dream then. That seems most odd to me.'

'Well, if it does happen again . . . ' William had answered, sounding far from comfortable, 'then maybe I'll have to believe it – at least while I'm here. But when I was away – at school – it just seemed . . . so unlikely. Surely you felt that? I couldn't go on thinking about it, because . . . I didn't believe in it.'

'Was it because you were frightened of it?' Mary had asked him.

'No!' he'd replied, sounding irritable.

'I was, last term,' Mary had said. 'I had to stop remembering it all because it scared me so much. Like . . . ' she'd paused, taking a deep breath, and when she'd next spoken her voice was no more than a whisper, ' . . . when I flew with the owl . . . '

'But – wasn't it wonderful, Mary? You must remember that?' Alice had insisted.

'It was the most frightening thing that's ever happened to me,' Mary had whispered, and she'd shivered and shaken her head. 'Let's play hide and seek,' she'd said, changing the subject, and no

9

matter how Alice tried, she couldn't get either of them to talk any more about it.

'I think you've been magicked,' she'd told them crossly. 'I think a spell has been cast on you so that you behave like this . . . '

'Oh, Alice!' William had wailed, putting his compass into his pocket, 'there are no such things as spells,' and before Alice had had a chance to protest he'd held up a hand, 'I agree with Mary,' he'd said, 'let's play hide and seek!'

2
'Kee! Kee!'

'Ninety eight, ninety nine, ONE HUNDRED!' Mary's voice rose to a crescendo. 'I'm coming!'

By moving her head a little, Alice could just see her sister standing at the bottom of the hill on the narrow forest track. She saw Mary slowly turn and scan her surroundings, with her eyes shaded by her hands against the glare of the sun which came and went as clouds chased across it, carried on the spring breeze.

The object of the game was for the hiders to get home to the tree stump and touch it, shouting 'block, one, two, three!' as they did so. Mary's job, as the seeker, was to stop them. She had first to discover their hiding place. Then, once they were seen, she had to intercept them before they could get to the home block and then she had to stop them, by touching them, like in tag. It should have been quite easy. All she had to do was to stay by the block until someone approached and then chase them. But, as soon as she chased one person, she would have to leave the block unguarded. This was the best time for another player to creep in, unobserved. The best strategy for a hider, therefore, was to get as close to the block as possible without being seen and then to make a dash for it while the seeker's attention was distracted.

Alice decided at once that she had hidden herself too far away from the block. But to go back to the lower track by the way she had come was impossible now that Mary had finished counting. The hillside up which she had scrambled was covered by grasses, ferns, young bracken, huge clumps of brambles and spiky wild roses with only a few stunted bushes to hide behind. If she tried to return that way, Mary would be sure to see her. She looked round for an alternative route. What she needed was some cover.

A narrow track, no more than a muddy indentation in the grass, led away from her, winding behind the gorse bushes, then across a bit of open land, before entering the deeper woods that crowded in on either side of the clearing in which she was crouching. If she could reach the protection of the trees, she reckoned, she'd easily be able to work her way down to the bottom of the bank without being seen. The only problem would be crossing the open ground.

Glancing back down the hill she could see Mary walking slowly along the track in the direction that William had taken and was now hiding. From Alice's vantage point she could see him standing behind a tree, just off the track. He obviously couldn't see Mary because, once, he moved slowly round the trunk to get a better look, then pulled back quickly, apparently surprised by how close she was to his hiding place.

Then, just as Mary might have discovered him,

a movement on the other side of the track made her swing round.

'Spot!' she yelled. 'I can see you!' and the dog, hearing his name being called, came bounding out of the undergrowth, barking and jumping round her. Taking advantage of this distraction, William broke his cover, making a dash back along the track towards the block.

'William!' Mary yelled. 'I can see you!'

'You've got to tag me, Mary!' her brother shouted, without looking back, as he ran for the block.

Spot, seeing William racing away, thought this was a much better game and ran after him, jumping round his feet, slowing him up and forcing him off the track once more, back in amongst the trees.

'Spot!' William yelled, laughing. 'You're not supposed to do this. You're not on Mary's side . . .'

Mary was charging at William now, her arms flung out as she tried to touch him. All the time Spot wound between them, barking and jumping, his tail wagging and his paws reaching out to them both.

While Mary was distracted, Alice turned and sprinted along the path, crouching low behind the gorse bushes and then even lower as she passed out of their protection on to the bare hillside, in full sight of the path below. But Mary and William and Spot had now all tumbled together into a heaving, kicking, laughing and barking heap and were completely unaware of her.

In front of her a line of fir trees blocked the way. They had been planted so closely together that, at first, she thought she wouldn't be able to squeeze between them. But the path she was on wound round a first tree – its graceful boughs, covered in dark green needles, reaching almost to the ground – and then passed through a gap between two other trunks that until then had been invisible.

At once she was in the gloomy interior of the forest. After the bright, blowy, day outside, it was like entering another world. Here the light was filtered, brown and dim, through a thick web of needle-less branches. The only sign of life on the trees was right at the top, where their green tips stretched for a sky that could only be guessed at from below. The ground was covered with years and years of dropped needles and dry cones. Scarcely any plants grew on the sour earth and those that did were thin and rank; a few ferns, a straggle of ivy, long thorny tendrils of bramble and, in one place, some almost-black and evil looking toadstools. But it was the stillness that Alice noticed most. The breeze, which outside had been fresh and invigorating, was reduced to a dull, distant roar as it forced its way through the mesh of interwoven branches and twigs. There were no birds singing. Even Spot's barking and William and Mary's laughing voices disappeared at once, as though they had ceased to exist. The air, which had smelt clean and sparkling, was here thick and dank with decay.

The path became more difficult to follow. The ground was strewn with rotting branches and some whole, fallen trees – jammed in and balanced crazily amongst the rows of upright trunks. There were occasional mounds of loose stones, covered with moss and dull lichen and sudden ridges of rough, dark rock jutting up out of the earth.

Rounding one of these outcrops, she was surprised to find that the ground fell away from her, almost sheer, down into a gloomy hollow where the trees were packed so tightly together that they appeared like a solid wall of trunks, too close even for her to slip between.

Alice turned back and started to retrace her steps to the side of the forest from which she had entered. She didn't at all like this dead, half-world that she'd strayed into, she decided, and would be glad to be back on the outside. But now the way looked completely unfamiliar; or rather, the very sameness of the view ahead made her unsure of precisely which route she had taken. She followed a narrow, beaten track – made, she supposed, by an animal – which led her more gradually up hill until, in front of her through the gloom, she could just make out some green shrubs and a sudden shaft of sunlight cutting through the trees. She hurried forward, hoping that she might have reached the side of the forest, and the open ground beyond, but when she reached the light, she found only a clump of holly bushes and a carpet of long, thin grasses where a few trees had been chopped down many years before. She could see the trunks piled in a mouldering heap at the side of the glade. All around her, the dark and silent forest pressed in, stifling her with its presence.

She turned slowly in a full circle, searching for any familiar object that would tell her which way to go. But there was none. Wherever she looked, the same ranks of trees stretched away from her into the gloom. She had no idea now from which direction she had started out; she had no idea in which direction to continue.

Alice was lost.

'William!' she called, fighting back the panic that she could feel welling up from her stomach, making her heart beat faster and a lump of tears form in the back of her throat.

'William? Mary?' she shouted, louder this time. Then she paused, waiting, without much hope, for an answering call.

The silence that surrounded her was almost throbbing. It seemed solid, like the great circle of trees that hemmed her in. She shouted again, but her voice sounded unfamiliar. It was like shouting into a pillow; muffled and lifeless.

'William!' she yelled. And, 'Mary!'

She made the words as long and as loud as she could. But no answering call came back to her; only an awful stillness and a terrible, booming nothing.

At last Alice sat down on the pile of logs and stuffed her hands into the pockets of her anorak. She tried to calm herself and work out the direction in which she had come. She thought of William bragging about his compass but realized that even if she had one it wouldn't be much use because she didn't know which way she should be heading. She thought that if she retraced her steps back into the forest to the outcrop of rock then she might, perhaps, find her original path but now, with a gasp of fear, she realized that she wasn't even sure which way she had entered the clearing in which she was sitting.

'Oh, help!' she whispered and she looked up to where a patch of clear sky glittered with light above her head. There the tops of the firs tossed and swayed in the breeze and clouds raced across the blue. It was like looking through a keyhole from a dark cupboard at the bright world outside.

Alice took a deep breath and pursed her lips. It occurred to her that the easiest and most obvious way out of her predicament would be to fly. But of course that wasn't possible. Unless;

'If only the Magician would come,' she thought. 'He could help me.'

A faint speck on the blue sky wheeled round and round above her head, gradually forming into a bird as it flew closer to the surface of the trees.

Alice felt, in some peculiar way, that it was looking at her. Or, at least, as it was the only sign of life, she hoped that it could see her. She stretched out her hand to it, willing the bird not to fly away out of her sight. She saw it stretch its wings, like a swimmer treads water, and hover on the invisible air. She heard it cry out; a long, plaintive 'Kee kee' sound. Then it reached its claws downwards and dropped like a stone, to land, with a great flapping of wings, on one of the highest branches of a fir. There it settled and slowly arched its neck, peering down at her.

For a moment neither of them moved.

The eyes of the bird were like pinpricks of light. They seemed to hold Alice in their piercing gaze so that she was transfixed. But she didn't feel afraid. It wasn't an unfriendly stare, but cool and interested; the enquiring look of a scientist through a microscope or of an artist seeing his subject.

'Please,' Alice whispered, 'I'm a bit lost.'

'Kee kee!' the bird called. The sound had a dying fall. It reminded her of high moors and lonely landscapes. A cold sound. It made her shiver. She dug her hands deeper into her pockets and bit her lower lip.

'I was with my brother and sister,' she continued, feeling that one of them had to make some attempt at conversation. 'We were playing hide and seek . . . '

'Kee! Kee!' the bird called.

'You're not by any chance connected to the Magician, are you?' Alice said.

The bird darted its head forward then turned it sharply to the side, as though it was listening.

Alice, released from its stare, turned quickly to look in the same direction and, as she did so, she heard Spot barking.

'Spot!' she shouted, jumping up off the log and running in the direction of the sound. 'Spot! I'm here. Spot!'

As the excited barking grew closer, Alice glanced up at the tree once more. The bird stretched its wings and launched itself into the air.

'I'll be all right now,' Alice called. 'That's my friend, Spot, you can hear. He'll show me the way.'

'Kee! Kee!' the bird called and then slowly it circled the sky above the clearing and a moment later disappeared from view.

3
The Two Paths

It was Spot who first noticed that Alice was missing. William and Mary were sitting on the side of the track, gasping for breath after all the exertion of fighting, when he suddenly raised his head, his nostrils twitching, and raked the distant high ground behind them with his eyes.

'What Spot?' Mary asked. 'Did you see Alice?' and she sprang to her feet, turning at the same time, and calling out: 'Come on out, Alice. We can all see you.'

'You liar, Mary!' William said, also rising. 'You can't see her at all.' Then he frowned. 'I wonder where she is.'

'Still hiding,' Mary answered, searching the tree line with her eyes. 'You know Alice. She never gives in.'

'But she's had masses of chances to get to the block – while we were fighting,' William said and, as he spoke, he started to run after Spot, who was already half way up the bank, his nose to the ground, following Alice's scent.

Spot soon reached the place behind the gorse bush, where Alice had crouched. He could smell her strongly here. He wagged his tail, yelping and barking as he searched the ground with his nose. Then he lifted his head, one front paw raised off the ground, and looked towards the distant trees. As he did so, his tail went down between his legs and he started to whine pitifully.

'What is it, Spot? What's the matter?' William asked, catching him up and putting a comforting hand on the back of his neck. Then he also looked towards the bank of firs, rising like a rampart in front of them.

'What's up?' Mary asked, panting as she ran up the hill to join them.

'I don't know,' William said. 'It's Spot. Something's upsetting him.'

As he spoke, Spot whined, turning round and round, as though he was reluctant to proceed.

'There's something wrong, Mare,' William whispered, and he knelt down on the ground in front of the dog. 'What is it, boy?' he asked, his voice sounding gentle. 'Is it Alice? Is she in danger?'

Spot's whining turned to yelping and he jumped up and down, then turned and started to walk, with obvious reluctance, towards the trees.

'He doesn't want to go in there,' Mary said, in a puzzled voice. Then she added, 'Oh, Will! I wish the magic would start.'

'I thought you were afraid of it,' William mumbled, as though still not wanting to admit to the possibility.

'If the magic would start – Spot could talk to us. That's all I meant,' Mary replied.

'You think it really happened, then?' William asked.

'I know it did,' Mary answered him. 'And so do you, really. You do, don't you?'

William sighed.

'Yes,' he answered her. 'But not like Alice does; I'm not sure, like she is. I find it easier to believe now we're here, I suppose. But, at school, it all seemed so . . . improbable.'

He looked at the dog. Spot was lying on the ground again, with his front paws stretched out in front of him, staring at the trees.

'You don't want to go in there, do you?' William said to him gently, scratching him behind an ear. The dog looked up sideways at him and whimpered.

'Is Alice in there?' Mary asked, crouching down on the other side of Spot and putting an arm round his shoulders. The dog's whining became louder and more anguished.

William and Mary stared at each other.

'We'll have to go, won't we?' Mary said, at last.

William shrugged.

'I don't mind,' he said. 'It's just a few trees. I'm not scared. Are you?'

Mary shook her head, thoughtfully.

'Spot is, though', she replied. 'Come on,' she said, gently, to the dog. 'If Alice is in danger, we'll have to, Spot. But I'd much rather you were with us. Please.'

The dog rose slowly and licked her hand. Then it turned, sniffing the ground, and started to walk, head down and tail wagging slowly, towards the trees, following the route that Alice had taken.

The gloom of the forest settled round them like

a blanket. They had to walk in single file, following Spot who sniffed the ground and the trunks and even the air in front of him in his effort to pick up Alice's scent.

'The difficulty is the needles absorb the smell,' Mary called over her shoulder to William who was following her. 'It makes following her much harder.'

William touched his sister on the shoulder.

'How did you know that?' he asked her, in a half whisper.

Mary stopped and looked back at him, puzzled and frowning.

'I don't know,' she answered. 'The idea just came into my head,' and, as she spoke she swung round, looking at Spot who was still prowling along ahead of her.

'Spot?' she called, stopping the dog in his tracks.

'What?' Spot asked.

'You're talking to us,' Mary exclaimed. 'Did you hear him, Will?'

William nodded, not taking his eyes off Spot.

'You're talking to us, Spot,' Mary said again, reaching out and stroking his head.

'Not really,' Spot replied. 'I'm just thinking.'

'But . . . we know what you're thinking. It's the magic, isn't it? It's the Magician letting it happen,' and she looked around, impatiently, searching among the dense trees for a glimpse of him. 'Oh, where is he?' she sighed. 'I do wish he'd come.'

'He doesn't always come when we need him,' Spot told her. 'Sometimes we have to work things out for ourselves.' But as the dog thought this, he looked round also as if he too wished that Stephen Tyler, the Magician, would appear.

'So – if Stephen Tyler isn't making this happen . . . ' William said, using his working out voice. Then he stopped speaking.

'What, Will?'

'We must be doing it ourselves.'

'Doing what?' Mary asked him, impatiently.

'Hearing Spot . . . it isn't magic. It's . . . something we're doing . . . because we believe we can.'

'That's the secret of magic,' Spot said, 'believing', and he growled the word, quietly.

'Yes,' William said, thinking deeply. 'But, in order to believe, you have to sort of . . . give up questioning. It's more like . . . stopping *not* believing. When I was at school, I couldn't believe what had happened here . . . because none of it made sense. I asked myself questions and . . . couldn't believe the answers. I didn't believe . . . you see?'

'Well, let's start believing that we can find Alice,' Mary suggested. 'I don't like this forest any more than Spot does,' and she shouted: 'Alice? Alice, where are you? Alice?'

The sound of her voice was lost amongst the trees.

'Which way, Spot?' William asked.

The dog looked round, sniffing the air and listening, his head on one side, his ears pricked forward, the hair on the back of his neck standing up.

'That's the trouble with this place,' he growled. 'It's dead.'

23

'Dead?' Mary asked, looking round at the tall, brown trunks.

'Oh, the trees are still living,' Spot replied. 'But they're not natural. This forest used to be all bright and light. You've never seen so many shades of green as there were here. All this ground was covered with bluebells in spring, and grass that was sweet to eat. There were berries and butterflies. . . . The sun used to shine here through the branches and it was lovely and cool in summer. In autumn the leaves fell and covered the ground with a red and brown carpet – colour like you've never seen. Then, when the winter snow came, it was piled up so deep in some places that it was all you could do to get through it.'

'But that must have been ages ago, Spot,' William said, following the dog as it continued to snuffle along in front of them. 'Long before your lifetime. I mean these trees must have been here for years.'

Spot looked over his shoulder and growled.

'There you go again,' he said. 'Working out.'

William frowned and was silent. It was all very well, he thought. But that was what humans were good at – using their brains. That's what made them the superior animal.

'If humans are superior,' Spot replied, without looking back at him, 'how come they managed to make such a mess of the forest, then? Most of the creatures who lived here . . . have gone now.' And he said the last words with such a sigh that Mary shivered.

'I don't see how you can blame humans,' William said. 'They had to use the forest, just like farmers use the land.'

'But they took away the right trees and planted these instead,' Spot growled. 'These aren't the sort of trees that used to live here. They chose them because they grow faster, that's all. Birds don't nest in them; plants won't grow under them; nothing lives here . . .'

They came to a place where a cliff of rock jutted out in front of them, with the ground falling away steeply on either side. Spot led them to the edge of rock, where it thrust forward, breaking out of the tree line as if it was heading straight for the sky. Below and all around them the forest stretched to the horizon. The tips of the firs revealed the straight lines in which they'd been planted.

'It's like a grid,' Mary said, thinking out loud. And it was true. From their viewpoint, there was such a neat, ordered aspect to the forest. All the trees were of a uniform height and they followed the contours of the land beneath them in such strict, unvarying lines.

Then William pointed.

'Look over there,' he said.

The distant hillside which he indicated sprang up out of the landscape, billowing with a froth of green and white.

'Blossom,' said Mary, delighted with the sight of it.

'Real trees,' said William.

'How it used to be,' said Spot.

'Can we go there one day?' asked Mary.

'You can go anywhere,' replied the dog. 'Only it's best not to go alone and it's best not to stray too far from the known paths.'

And the children remembered Alice again.

'Help,' murmured Mary. 'She could be any-where.' Then she gasped. 'Hey!' she said, 'isn't that a sort of a path down there?' and, as she spoke, she pointed to where a brown line cut between the trees, straight as an arrow. This cleft climbed the steep escarpment further along from where they were standing and then disappeared out of sight in amongst the trees behind them.

'And there's another one over there,' said William, pointing to where, distantly, a sliver of paler green parted the dull uniformity of the forest. This narrow ride also climbed up to their level and then was lost in the trees behind them.

'The light path and the dark path,' growled Spot. 'You must never go down the dark path. Not ever.'

'Where does it lead?' asked Mary, staring at the straight brown track.

'Deeper and deeper into the forest. It's not a good place. We never go there.'

'And the other one?' asked William, looking at the green way.

'It goes deeper into the forest as well.'

'Is that one safe?'

'You must ask the Magician,' Spot replied.

'The Magician,' said Mary wistfully. 'If only he was here. We're never going to find Alice in all those trees. She could be anywhere.'

'Isn't there any way we can call him up, Spot?' William asked.

'Oh, so you believe in him again now, do you?' the dog said, looking up at him with unblinking, staring, eyes.

'I didn't not believe in him,' William protested,

26

sounding a bit peeved. 'It was just . . . oh, I can't explain to a dog. What am I doing talking to a dog, anyway? The guys at school would think I was off my rocker.'

'Is that what you think?' Spot asked. 'That you're off your rocker?'

'No, he doesn't,' Mary said firmly, cutting in before William had a chance to reply. 'Now please, Spot, answer William's question. Is there any way that we can call the Magician up? I mean make him come to us?'

'I dare say he'd come – if you needed him enough,' replied the dog. And, as he spoke, he looked up into the sky, his tail slowly beginning to wag.

'But how would we call him?' Mary insisted.

'You wouldn't,' Spot replied. 'He'd just arrive. . . . Listen!' and he barked the last word, straining forward with his head, one foot raised off the ground, as he listened to a distant sound.

'Kee! Kee!'

'What is it?' asked Mary, searching the sky for the source of this strange, sad, call.

'Kestrel,' said William. And as he spoke he saw the bird wheeling in the air far above them.

'Kee! Kee! Kee!' it cried again.

Then, as William and Mary watched, the hawk dropped out of the sky and disappeared from sight, down into the trees, somewhere behind them.

'Come on,' said Spot, setting off at a trot back into the forest.

'Where are we going?' asked William, following him.

'You really don't understand anything, do

you?' said Spot. Then he started to bark and a moment later, distantly but distinctly, they heard a voice, calling their names.

'That's Alice,' said Mary excitedly.

'Of course it is,' said Spot. 'Come on.'

'But which way?' insisted William.

'Kee! Kee! Kee!' the Kestrel called, appearing above the trees once more. And, as they watched, it slowly circled, higher and higher, its mournful call growing fainter as its shape gradually merged into the blue of the sky.

'Mr Tyler!' William shouted involuntarily, and as he did so, he ran forward, stretching out his hands in front of him, as if willing the bird not to depart.

'Where?' asked Mary, looking round hopefully.

'The Kestrel,' William replied.

'But – it's gone,' said Mary.

'William! Mary! Spot!' Alice's voice sounded, nearer to them now.

'He showed us where she was,' said William quietly.

'Oh,' said Mary. 'Then he did come to help us.'

Ahead of them Spot was barking excitedly as he dodged between the trunks and across the soft brown ground, making for the distant glint of green where a thin ray of sunlight was showing them the clearing where Alice was waiting for them.

4
Brock

They found Alice sitting on a pile of logs at the side of the clearing, her hands stuck into the pockets of her anorak, looking really fed up.

'What took you so long getting here?' she demanded, reproachfully.

'Honestly, Alice!' Mary snapped. 'You could at least show a bit of gratitude.'

'I've been lost in this stupid wood for hours,' her sister said and she kicked the ground in front of her petulantly.

Mary and William exchanged a look and remained silent. There were times when Alice's moods were better left unchallenged.

'We're not out of here yet,' Spot growled, sounding far from confident, as though he knew they were still lost.

But at the sound of his voice Alice jumped up delightedly, her mood changing at once.

'Spot!' she exclaimed, forgetting all about her misery and fear. 'Oh, Spot! You just talked!'

'So?' the dog asked her wearily.

'Well, you wouldn't earlier. You didn't say a thing to me. No matter how much I pleaded.'

'I was talking to you all the time,' the dog growled. 'You just weren't listening.'

'Not listening!' Alice protested. 'I wanted you to talk to me more than anything in the world.'

'Well then, you weren't listening properly,' the dog replied, gruffly. 'I could hear you. But you were so busy trying to make me answer you that you missed it when I did.'

Then, seeing how dejected his reprimand made Alice look, he felt sorry at once and nuzzled his nose into her hand and licked her palm.

Alice stroked the dog's head as he sat on the ground in front of her, with his nose on her knee. William and Mary came and sat on the pile of logs beside her. They were all silent, lost in their own thoughts.

'It really is very odd,' Alice said at last, looking at her brother and sister. 'Not at all how I imagined. I mean . . . I thought we'd come back to Golden House . . . and the magic would start . . . and the Magician would be here . . . '

'He was here,' William told her, sadly. As he spoke he looked up at the patch of blue sky above their heads.

'Where?' Alice cried.

'William thinks the bird was Stephen Tyler,' Mary told her.

'Which bird?' Alice demanded.

'The one that flew above the clearing here,' Mary replied.

'The kestrel,' William said, quietly.

'You saw it?' Alice asked.

Mary nodded.

'It was as if it was showing us where you were,'

she told Alice. 'At least, it was just after seeing the bird that we heard you calling.'

'I don't think that bird was Stephen Tyler!' Alice said. 'It really scared me. Like those things in the desert . . . What are those birds called that wait for people to die?'

'Vultures,' Mary replied.

'Well, it had that sort of look to me,' Alice said. 'It had really peculiar eyes. They seemed to stare right into me. I'm sure it was waiting to eat me.'

'But that's it,' William said. 'Don't you remember? That's how the fox used to look. . .,. Really deep.'

'And the owl,' Mary agreed.

Then they all turned and looked at Spot, who glared back at them with the same, unblinking stare.

'And Spot,' Alice said quietly. 'You stare like that as well. Does that mean the Magician is in you now? Is he, Spot?'

But the dog merely put his head on one side and wagged his tail a little.

'Sometimes,' Mary said, thoughtfully, 'it's as if he's just an ordinary dog, isn't it?'.

'Well, maybe that's because I am,' Spot growled. 'Just ordinary. It's you lot who're strange, not me!' And the dog yawned and stretched his legs out in front of him and licked one of his feet.

They were silent again. All around them the forest watched and waited.

'Oh!' Alice said at last, shivering as she spoke, 'I really hate this place.'

'Yes,' William agreed. 'We'd better get going. It must be nearly lunch time.' Then he turned, looking slowly round the glade. 'But . . . which way, Spot?' he asked.

Spot also looked round, sniffing the air.

'Oh, fishcakes!' Alice said, scratching her cheek. 'I'm really hungry now.'

'It's quite late,' actually, Mary said looking at her watch.

Alice hadn't got a watch. Or rather she had had one. It had been given to her by her Mum and Dad for Christmas one year. But it had never kept very good time and, after they'd had it repaired a few times, it was decided that she was one of those people who couldn't wear a watch because they had too much electricity in their bodies. She'd tried lighting a lamp bulb by rubbing it in her hair after this revelation – but with no success. The most she could achieve was a mild electric shock from the car door or a crackling sound when she took off her school shirt, neither of which phenomenon, even she had to admit, was exactly a world-shattering scientific breakthrough. However, as far as knowing the hours of the day was concerned, she claimed that her stomach was as good as any watch and that by it she could always tell precisely what time it was.

'It is now lunchtime,' she announced, 'and I'm really hungry. I could eat at least seven sausages.' Sausages were her favourite food. 'Oh, Spot!' she wailed, 'please get us out of here,' and she crossed to where the dog was sniffing the ground with immense interest and put an arm round his neck.

'Badger!' Spot said, looking up at her and grinning. Then they both turned back and snuffled the ground again with their nose.

At once Alice could smell the sharp, acrid scent. It was so strong that, for a moment, she thought she was going to be sick. She pulled away from the dog and turned to face William and Mary.

'Oh!' she shuddered. Then, realizing what had just taken place, she sat back on her haunches.

'William!' she whispered. 'It just happened again!'

'What did?' He sounded a bit irritable. William didn't like being lost. He felt it cast a slight on his manliness and made him look a bit wet. These problems had only recently begun to affect him; in fact until almost this precise moment being manly and not being wet had not mattered to him a scrap. But now, for some unaccountable reason, he felt personally insulted by the predicament in which they found themselves. He was therefore in no mood to listen to Alice, who had jumped up off the logs and was facing them both, her face alight with excitement.

'I went inside Spot,' she said. 'I smelt through his nose!'

'Oh, Alice!' William groaned, dismissively.

'But I did, Will,' Alice protested.

'No you didn't,' Mary said. 'I was watching you the whole time. You just knelt down beside him.'

'I smelt through his nose, Mary,' Alice insisted. 'I really did. Like before. You remember? Like when you flew with the owl . . . '

'I was watching you, Alice,' Mary told her. 'You just knelt down beside him.'

Then, before Alice had a chance to reply, Spot

33

suddenly bounded forward, his tail wagging and his nose close to the ground.

'Come on,' he barked. 'This way.'

The children had to run to keep up with him. They dodged round trees and pushed through branches. They crossed occasional dingy glades, similar to the one that Alice had found. Sometimes they had to skirt round pools of dark, stagnant water or jump across sodden tracks, oozing with mud. They slithered down into hollows and climbed, panting, up steep banks. All the time the brown, half-light engulfed them and the motionless trees surrounded them on all sides. The only sounds were their own footsteps as they pounded the dank earth and snapped dead twigs under their feet.

At last they came to a place where a broad path cut across their way. Here the trees, which leaned together across the divide, were festooned with creeper and the ground beneath them was carpeted with rank weeds and rotting wood. Lurid toadstools grew out of the decaying stumps of trees and dead branches stuck up out of the undergrowth, like the blackened bones of animals.

Spot stopped at the side of this track. He paced up and down in the space between two trees, without putting a foot into the opening in front of him. The hairs on his neck stood up, bristling with apprehension. A low growl rolled in the back of his throat. His tail hung low and swished angrily.

'What is it, boy?' William whispered, sensing the dog's unease.

'Don't you feel it?' Spot growled, not taking his eyes off the track in front of them.

34

William looked round. He could see nothing unusual.

'Feel what?' he asked, and, as he spoke, he walked out of the shelter of the trees into the centre of the track.

Spot barked once, springing back away from the track and knocking into Mary who was standing just behind him.

'What's the matter?' she said, putting a hand on the back of his neck to steady him. The dog trembled beside her.

'Come on,' William called. 'It'd be easier walking up this track. It must lead somewhere.'

'No!' Spot barked. 'It isn't a good place.'

'Is it the track we saw from the cliff?' Mary asked, suddenly feeling shivery. 'The one you called the Dark Path?'

'You must feel it,' Spot pleaded with them.

'I do feel a bit . . . cold,' Mary said at last.

'But it's no worse than the rest of this vile forest,' William called.

Only Alice remained silent. She hung back away from the side of the track and put her hands back into her pockets for comfort.

'You feel something, don't you?' Spot said to her, pushing his nose up close to her.

'It's true I don't like it very much,' she told him, in a small voice. 'What is this place, Spot?'

'The Dark and Dreadful Path,' the dog said, quietly. 'No animals come here. Not from choice.' Then he sniffed the ground again, puzzled. 'But Badger crossed here,' he said at last, and he lifted his head, staring across the track to the woods beyond. Then, eerily and unexpectedly, he let out a long, high wail. It was the sort of howl a wolf might make in the night, chilling and sad.

'Oh, Spot,' Alice cried, throwing her arms round his neck to comfort him. 'What's the matter?' And she felt so full of love for the dog that it made her want to cry.

A moment later William found the reason for the dog's distress. At the other side of the track, he discovered, partially hidden by a mound of loose twigs and undergrowth, the lifeless body of a badger. It was as though the creature had tried to crawl into the mound for warmth and protection. There was blood on the back of its neck and it looked as though it had been attacked by some ferocious animal.

'Oh!' William called out, aghast. Then he turned his back, not wanting to look at the pitiful sight any more.

'What is it?' Alice asked, running forward.

'Don't look,' William said, stopping her. 'It's a badger, I think. Only it's dead.'

Spot ran quickly across the track to where the body lay. He nosed at it sadly, whimpering as he did so.

'Brock,' he cried, giving the sound the most tragic air. Then he barked loudly, angrily, and he snarled at the surrounding forest, as though, in some strange way, he blamed the trees or the place they were in for the fate of the badger. 'It's happening again,' he growled. 'It's happening again,' and, still muttering and barking he set off once more into the forest on the other side of the track.

'Well, come on,' the dog yelped, 'if you want to get back for feeding,' and it disappeared from view amongst the trees. Mary hurried across the track, joining William and Alice.

'I've never seen a badger before,' she said, staring at the lifeless body.

'How did it die?' Alice asked, in a sad voice.

'I think it's been attacked,' William said.

'Poor thing,' Alice sobbed, fighting back tears. 'I don't like this forest at all, William,' and she reached out and took hold of his hand.

'I don't like it much either,' her brother agreed.

'Come on,' Spot barked impatiently in the distance. 'There's a way down here.'

'We'd better go,' Mary said. 'We don't want to be late on our first day,' and she followed the sound of the dog's barking.

As William pulled her away, Alice gave one last, lingering, look at the dead badger, then, hand in hand, they hurried away from the Dark and Dreadful path.

5
The Writing on the Floor

Phoebe was at the range, stirring a pan, when they came in.

'There you are,' she said, looking up. 'Did you have a good walk? Lunch is nearly ready.'

William hurried upstairs and Alice went in search of Jack who was 'somewhere in the house,' Phoebe told them. 'I'm never quite sure where. I get hoarse shouting for him, sometimes. Tell him lunch is on the table, will you?'

Stephanie was in her cot and woke up suddenly at the sound of their voices. Mary crossed to her and, without asking for permission, picked her up and hugged her.

'That's your godmother, Steph,' Phoebe said, transferring the contents of the saucepan into a large bowl. 'Do you remember Mary?'

'I don't suppose she does,' Mary said, shyly.

'Well, she certainly should!' Phoebe exclaimed, setting cutlery and putting a large loaf of bread on a board in the middle of the table. 'Without your help, she'd have had a hard job coming into this world.'

'Oh, Stephanie!' Mary said and she rocked her in her arms. She felt suddenly overwhelmed with sadness and tears welled up in her eyes.

'What's the matter?' Phoebe asked, immediately concerned.

'Nothing,' Mary said, fighting back the tears. 'We saw a dead badger, that's all.'

Phoebe frowned and pushed some stray hairs away from her forehead.

'Oh, dear!' she exclaimed. 'How upsetting for you all. But that's nature, isn't it? The forest must be full of life and death.' She shivered. 'I sometimes feel it all around me. So much life, so much striving to survive, so much hunting and killing.' Then she shrugged, as though ridding herself of an unpleasant thought. 'Nature is cruel – if you think death is cruel. But then, in another way, it's all part of a cycle, isn't it? I expect, if we only knew where to look, we'd find a baby badger right now, just starting out in life – like Steph here – with everything ahead. I sometimes look at her and I'm . . . overwhelmed with how ready and expectant she is. How tough she is, really.' She crossed and put an arm round Mary. 'Don't be sad. Please.'

'I'm not,' Mary told her, embarrassed by this unexpected show of affection. 'Should I put her back in the cot?'

'Yes,' Phoebe told her. 'I'll feed her later.'

Alice and Jack came in, both of them giggling.

'Uncle Jack, Uncle Jack. What's yellow and stupid?' Alice yelled.

'I don't know. I don't know,' Jack exclaimed, raising his hands in a gesture of surrender.

'Thick custard!' Alice told him and she started to giggle again.

'That's pathetic, Alice,' Mary said. 'It's also very old.'

Alice shrugged.

'Uncle Jack hadn't heard it.'

'Where's William?' Phoebe asked.

'Gone to the loo, I expect. I'll get him,' Alice said, going out into the hall again and then, a moment later, they all heard her yelling his name at the top of her voice.

Eventually, when William arrived downstairs, they sat down to lunch. Phoebe had made a thick vegetable stew which she called a *ratatouille*.

'But I thought you were a vegetable-arian, Phoebe,' Alice protested.

'It is vegetables!' Phoebe told her.

'Not it's not. It's rat!' Alice said, giggling again and tucking into her food.

William and Mary exchanged a pained look.

'She gets like this sometimes,' William explained.

'Did you have a good walk?' Jack asked them.

'Yes, OK. We got a bit lost. Did you remember the map, Phoebe?' William asked.

'I didn't go into town in the end. I'll go in tomorrow. Sorry.'

'Doesn't matter,' William told her.

'Spot showed us the way home,' Alice said.

'What did you see? What did you do?' Jack asked, cutting slices of bread.

'A dead badger,' Mary told him, quetly. 'I think we should have buried it,' she added, addressing the remark to William and Alice.

40

'We couldn't. We didn't have a spade or anything.'

'I don't like to think of it, just left there,' Mary insisted.

'Oh, shut up, Mary. I don't want to think about it,' Alice told her, glumly.

'Maybe we could, tomorrow,' William said, thoughtfully.

'What?' Alice asked.

'Bury it,' he replied.

'I don't want to go back there,' Alice said, looking down and not meeting any of their eyes.

'I think Will's right,' Mary said. 'I vote we bury the poor thing.'

'I'm not sure about that,' Phoebe cut in, looking nervously at Jack. 'It could be full of disease by now and besides, the natural thing would be to leave it alone. It'll probably provide food for other creatures.'

'Oh, how disgusting!' Alice exclaimed. 'I can't bear to think of that.'

'Maybe you should become a vegetable-arian, Alice,' Phoebe said, with a twinkle in her eye.

Alice pouted and looked down at her plate again. She had a feeling that Phoebe was laughing at her and she didn't like it.

'You don't find sausages lying about in the forest,' she said crossly. 'And if you did, I'd be the first to eat them.'

'Not raw, Alice?' William exclaimed.

'Oh, shut up, William,' his sister exclaimed.

'I tell you what,' Jack interrupted them. 'I'll come with you in the morning and we'll bury the badger together. How's that?'

The children all agreed enthusiastically, but Phoebe shook her head.

'You can count Steph and myself out. I've never seen a live badger in the wild so I don't want to see a dead one, thank you very much.'

'But we mustn't take too long over it,' Jack continued. 'I've masses of work to do and, at some time, I've got to go into town myself.'

'Have you?' Phoebe asked him. 'Can't I do whatever has to be done?'

'Not unless you want to face the bank manager,' Jack told her.

'No thank you!' Phoebe said firmly. 'If we're bankrupt, I'd rather you heard the news first.'

'What's bankrupt?' Alice asked.

'No money,' Phoebe said, with feeling.

'Well, we've still got some left,' Jack said, with a grin.

'Some being the operative word,' Phoebe told him.

'Oh, Uncle Jack, you're not really bankrupt, are you?' Mary asked anxiously.

'No!' Jack said. 'We've still got enough money invested to see us through the building period. Then . . . ' he mimed blowing a trumpet and tooted a fanfare, 'come next spring, if all goes according to plan, Golden House Country Hotel will open to an eager and appreciative public and we'll start making a modest, but comfortable, living! Only . . . the plan would be going more smoothly, if I could get the builders back.'

'Here we go again,' Phoebe groaned.

'What builders?' William asked.

'We had some builders who came and worked on the roof a few weeks ago,' Phoebe explained.

'Phoebe didn't like them,' Jack interrupted her. 'So I had to let them go.'

'Jack, that's not true,' Phoebe protested. 'There wasn't any more work for them – we can't afford them all the time.'

'Well, there's work for them now . . . ' Jack said.

'Then get them back,' Phoebe said sharply. 'I'm not stopping you.'

There was a moment's silence round the table. The children, sensing tension between Jack and Phoebe, felt awkward and embarrassed.

'I just said,' Phoebe continued after a moment, 'that they seemed to spend more time making mugs of tea in the kitchen than actually working . . . '

'They did a wonderful job on the roof,' Jack argued.

'Yes, that's true. I give in. Get them back.'

'Did you have to have the whole roof remade, Uncle Jack?' William asked, trying to change the subject.

'No. We were lucky. All the timbers were sound. We only needed the tiles re-hung. Whoever built this place, built it to last. After you've finished eating, I'll take you on the grand tour and show you what we've done.'

'Oooh, yes!' Alice said, eagerly.

'We've discovered all sorts of things,' Jack said.

'What sort of things?' William asked, nervously.

'I warn you,' Phoebe said, 'you're letting your-selves in for hours of lecturing on how the house was built and what every little nook and cranny was probably used for.'

'Nooks and crannies?' Mary asked, suspiciously. 'You mean . . . you've discovered the secret room, Uncle Jack?'

William reached with his foot under the table and kicked Mary, so that she gasped with pain.

'Ow! William,' she exclaimed.

'Sorry,' her brother said, without sounding in the least bit sorry.

'No, we haven't discovered a secret room or a secret passage,' Jack said, oblivious of the children's concern. 'At least, not yet. Of course, there's supposed to be one. But then no self-respecting house should be without one. The main part of the house was originally some sort of religious retreat. A place where the monks came for prayer and meditation. There's supposed to be a secret tunnel that leads from here to the abbey at Llangarren. But I can't think it's very likely. Llangarren is five miles the other side of the valley as the crow flies and straight through a solid chunk of mountain! I mean, what would the monks want a secret passage for anyway? They weren't doing anything wrong, coming on retreat. You only need a secret passage – or a secret room, come to that – if you have something to hide, don't you?'

'How d'you know about all this anyway?' William asked him.

'From my friend Miss Prewett, at the local museum. She comes up with all sorts of stories about the place.'

After they'd finished lunch. Jack took them on the promised tour of the house. To the right of the

44

hall were two big square rooms, with long windows looking out on to the front and side of the house. The doors to these rooms were from the hall on either side of the chimney. Above, were two further identical rooms, with doors off the galleried landing, opposite Phoebe and Jack's bedroom. These rooms, Jack explained, had been altered from the original Tudor design sometime during the late eighteenth century.

'Towards the end of the Georges. Apparently at that time the house was owned by a gentleman farmer, who saw himself as rather important – a bit stuck up, in fact – and he wanted a bit of modern architecture to show how rich and important he was! Funny to think that Georgian architecture was once 'modern' isn't it? Anyway, he just got the builders to stick on new front and side walls and bung in some of the latest sash windows! All the original Tudor beams are still there, behind the plaster. This front room will eventually be the hotel lounge and the back one will be the bar. Upstairs we'll make into bedrooms – with a bathroom fitted into each of them . . . I hope! I have yet to perfect the art of plumbing!'

To the left of the hall, and entered through a door on the same wall as the kitchen door, was a narrow and dark corridor that led into a warren of rooms of all shapes and sizes with oak beams and low ceilings and much smaller windows, some of them with tiny diamond shaped panes of glass between lead bars.

'This is how the other side of the hall would have been originally,' Jack continued, leading the way. 'We're going to open some of these rooms out to make the hotel dining room.' He showed them a second staircase leading up to other bedrooms. 'Eventually we'll move into this area ourselves,' he told them, 'so you'd better decide which room you each want.'

'Can we have one each?' Alice asked quickly. All her life she'd longed for a room of her own.

'You can have your own bathroom as well, if you like – but it costs more!' Jack joked, and he put an arm round her shoulder.

'But we won't have to pay,' she protested. 'We're family.'

'OK. You can do the washing up instead!' Jack told her. Then he paused by another door. 'And down here,' he said, opening the door with a flourish and revealing a steep staircase, 'are the cellars. Come and see?'

He switched on a light fixed to the side wall and led the way down to a narrow passage, with thick beams supporting the low ceiling. Off this passage were a number of store rooms, filled with piles of junk and rubble.

'Goodness knows what it all is,' Jack said. 'I've searched through one or two piles and as far as I can see it's just centuries of accumulated rubbish. Like this, for example:' and, as he spoke, he raised a battered and rusty bucket. 'Or this,' he added, dropping the bucket with a clatter and picking up a mouldering suitcase instead. As he raised it, the lid slowly swung open and a heap of rotting clothes fell out and landed on the floor in a cloud of dust. 'See what I mean?' he said, dropping the suitcase once more. 'These cellars have been used to dump all the junk in that people didn't want and couldn't be bothered to dispose of properly. Until now, that is. I'm going to get a skip and keep filling it until this place is clear. There's something a bit depressing about knowing that you're living on top of a rubbish dump! One thing's for sure – there isn't any treasure down here! Not so you'd notice anyway! That was another of Miss Prewett's stories. Apparently Golden House got its name because there's gold hidden here! I'd like to know where! I could certainly use a bit. Anyway, this place will one day be the wine cellar and the boiler room will be down here and I might even have a butler's pantry, where I can creep away for a quick nip at the brandy, while no one is watching!'

He led the way further along the dimly lit passage. At the end was another dark wooden door.

'But this,' he said, turning the iron handle, 'is the *pièce de résistance*,' and swung the door open and beckoned them through.

They stepped into darkness and, as they did so, the temperature dropped several degrees. The cellar rooms they had been in had been stuffy and warm, but here, suddenly, the air was chill and had a damp edge.

'Wait a minute while I find the switch,' Jack told them and they saw him feeling along the wall in the dim light that spilled in from the passage behind them.

'Ah!' he said at last and with a *click!* a number of overhead lights went on.

They were standing in a low, vaulted room with a stone flagged floor and square stone pillars that supported the rough, rounded arches of the roof.

'We're right under the central tower,' Jack explained in a hushed voice. 'This is the original medieval building. Maybe at one time it was a crypt. There must once have been a staircase down to here – but I can't find where it was. There is one curious thing, though – look over here,' he said, leading them to a far wall. 'See?'

He was pointing at a low arch of stones set into the wall with its centre filled in with stone blocks. The top of this arch was no higher than Alice's knees.

'It looks as if there was once a door here, at a lower level than the rest of the floor – or steps leading down perhaps to another floor below this one. Maybe that's where the secret passage is supposed to be. What d'you think? – but if so, it's not exactly secret, is it?'

But the children were hardly listening to Jack, for they had, all at the same time, seen that there were letters scratched on the stone floor just in front of the arch.

'Hey!' Jack said, bending down to get a closer look, 'someone's been writing on my floor! D'you suppose it's medieval graffiti? What does it say?'

Alice crouched down and stared at the roughly scratched letters.

'It says, "*The Fang was here*"!' she answered, then she looked up at them.

'The Fang?' Jack repeated. 'I'm sure that wasn't there the last time I came in here. Who on earth is The Fang d'you suppose?'

Mary shivered and looked over her shoulder. For a moment she felt as if they were being watched from one of the dark corners of the cellar.

48

'What happened to the rat, Uncle Jack?' she asked in a small voice.

'The rat?' Jack asked, puzzled.

'You remember. When we were here at Christmas, when Stephanie was being born . . . there was a rat.'

'Tell you the truth, I never did see that rat. I thought you and Phoebe made it up. Well it certainly hasn't been around to my knowledge. What made you think of that?' Jack asked.

'Well – rats have fangs, don't they?' Mary said.

Jack grinned.

'You think it popped down here and wrote us a message?' he said. 'Must be a very clever rat!'

But Mary didn't seem to think the idea funny at all. She frowned and turned away from the message.

'I'm cold,' she said. 'Can we go back upstairs now please?' and she hurried towards the door.

'Oooh,' Alice said, with a shiver, 'I'm freezing as well. Aren't you, Will?'

But William was already hurrying after Mary, out of the crypt.

'Yes, it is a bit nippy,' Jack said, walking with Alice to the door and switching off the light. 'I expect it'll be just the right temperature for storing wine!' and he swung the oak door closed behind them.

6
The Yew Tree

The following morning the children retraced their steps up the steep side of the valley, with Spot leading the way. Jack went with them, carrying a garden spade and some pairs of thick gardening gloves.

'I don't fancy lifting a dead badger with my bare hands,' he explained.

After a bit of searching they found once more the broad cleft through the fir forest that Spot had called the Dark and Dreadful Path. Although the day was bright and sunny, the same dismal light filled the place that they remembered from the previous day and the same oppressive atmosphere pervaded everything with its sense of sadness and decay.

'What a dreary bit of the woods,' Jack said, as he entered the open ride.

William led the way to where the dead badger still lay, half hidden under the mound of twigs. Spot hung back, with his tail between his legs and his head lowered.

'Poor old chap,' Jack exclaimed, examining the badger. 'It looks as though it's been in a fight. You see, there on the neck, where all the fur is torn.

Something pretty big must have attacked it,' and, as he spoke he looked up, his eyes searching the dense trees that surrounded them.

'Hurry, please, Uncle Jack,' Alice said, in a small voice. 'I really hate this bit of the forest.' And she also stayed back, standing next to Spot, not wanting to enter the clearing.

Jack dug a shallow trench at the side of the ride, in amongst a patch of bracken. Then, with William's help, he lowered the badger into it and scooped the earth once more over the top so that, eventually, the body was covered.

'D'you suppose we should say a prayer or something?' Mary whispered.

'Just "Rest In Peace", don't you think?' Jack answered, quietly.

Mary nodded and whispered the words under her breath.

'Oh, let's go away from here,' Alice pleaded, 'and never come back. I hate this place. And so does Spot.'

'All over now,' Jack said, breaking the mood. 'Like Phoebe said, this sort of thing is happening all the time out here. We mustn't be sad. It's all part of nature. OK? So – are you all coming back with me?'

'I'd quite like to try for the top of the valley,' William said. 'We saw real woods, yesterday, from a place where we got a view. D'you remember, Mary? They looked really nice. I'd quite like to go there, if we can.'

'I don't want to get lost again,' Alice protested.

'I think you should come back,' Jack said. 'At least until we have a proper map for you to use.'

'Oh, please, Uncle Jack. We won't get lost. I've got my bearings now. It was just confusing yesterday.'

'Well . . . ' Jack hesitated. 'Phoebe will never forgive me if you get lost again . . . '

'Please,' William pleaded.

'What about you, girls? D'you want to go exploring again?' Jack asked them.

Mary shrugged.

'Can if you like,' she said.

'Oh, all right then,' Alice said, giving in and trying not to show that she was really quite eager to 'go exploring' as Jack called it.

'We passed another path on the way up here,' Jack said. 'You could try there.'

They retraced their steps down the side of the valley to where the path Jack had spoken of veered off, leading upwards once more through the drab brown light of the fir forest.

'Back in time for lunch, mind,' Jack called after them, as they parted. 'And it's already well after eleven, so you haven't got long.'

'We won't go far,' William called.

Then, with Spot in the lead, the children started to climb the steep hillside, leaving behind them the Dark and Dreadful Path and the badger's burial mound.

Gradually, at first almost imperceptibly, the light began to change. The gloom beneath the trees was lifting, as thin rays from the invisible sun up above pierced the blanket of branches, making slanting patterns of light and shade that danced and flickered into the distance all around them.

Somewhere not far away, a bird began to sing.

The sound was so bright and cheerful that it lifted their spirits. Spot looked up, straining forward, and his tail started to wag for the first time since they'd left the dead badger.

The air was fresher now. They could feel the breeze on their skins; they could smell the faint perfume of flowers.

The sombre, evergreen firs gave way to leaf-shedding trees. The silver bark of birch mingled with the green-tinged trunks of sweet chestnut; the stately beech shared space with the weeping willow. Thin saplings grew in clumps and towering oaks reached above them to the sky. Pale spring buds decked all the branches and late catkins scattered golden pollen on the glossy leaves of trailing ivies. They came to a place where a drift of cherry blossom hung low across their path, its petals as white as driven snow.

The ground beneath their feet was springy with grass and the long spiky leaves of bluebells, not yet in flower. Wood anemones grew in profusion and cushions of primroses pushed up between the roots of the trees.

A squirrel, surprised by their sudden arrival, scuttled away from them, scrambling up into a spreading beech tree. They saw it, a moment later, leaping from branch to branch and tree to tree until, with a swish of its tail, it disappeared from view.

The ground was rising now. Soon they were panting for breath as they toiled up the steep incline. More and more birds were singing and they caught flashes of yellow and blue as tits and finches darted in the branches, catching gnats and grubbing for food under the bark and amongst the leaves. A sudden, dazzling green streak was followed a moment later by the drumming of a woodpecker, and the loud, clattering cry of a startled blackbird disturbed the peace.

At last, reaching the summit of the hill, they paused for breath. They were on the edge of a high escarpment. Beyond, the forest dropped away gently into a shallow valley, and then rose again towards the distant horizon. Behind them, back the way they had climbed, they were now high enough above the forest floor to be able to see the view.

They were looking down on Golden Valley. They could see the house, with the dovecote in the kitchen garden directly in front of it. Beyond the house, the side of the valley rose up almost like a cliff. The firs clung to the steep earth, green and thick. At the crest of this hill they were able to see, for the first time, a cleft in the forest. This gap in the trees was quite remarkable. It looked as if it had been cleared to accommodate a road.

'I didn't know there was a road up there,' William said, sounding puzzled.

'We've never been this high up before,' Mary said.

'Look at the mountains,' Alice whispered.

Above the tree line, through the gap in the forest, distant and dark against the paler sky, a ridge of higher hills was just visible. And as they stared at them, a shaft of light glinted on a distant summit.

'Isn't that odd . . . ?' William exclaimed.

'What, Will?' Mary asked.

'It's all in a straight line. Coincidence, I suppose.'

'What is?' Alice said.

'You see the summit of that highest peak?'

The girls both nodded.

'It's in a direct line with that gap in the trees. Then the chimneys of Golden House. Then the top of the dovecote . . . '

He stopped speaking, looking round eagerly. Behind them a huge yew tree – more like a yew copse it was so vast and many trunked – clung to the edge of the hill, blocking the immediate view. But going round behind it, William gasped.

'Look!' the girls heard him say and they hurried to see what it was that had so surprised him.

Not far from where they were standing, a single rough-hewn stone poked up out of the undergrowth. As tall as a man, it leaned slightly to one side as though at some time the ground under it had settled. A holly bush was growing beside it, half covering it, but it was clearly there.

'Like a marker,' William said, quietly.

'And look beyond, Will,' Mary exclaimed, running forward a few steps and pointing as she did so.

Deep in the woods, the sun was reflecting on a stretch of water.

'A lake,' Alice cried out. 'And after the lake – look! You see where the ground begins to rise again? There's another of those funny gaps in the trees . . . '

'And really big mountains beyond,' Mary said, pointing.

Through the gap, etched across the horizon,

the jagged peaks of high mountains could just be seen.

'That must be Wales,' William said and he turned slowly looking back across Golden Valley to the other gap in the trees. 'You see . . . ?' he said, speaking more to himself than to the others.

'All in a straight line,' Mary agreed, thoughtfully.

'I wonder how long this tree's been here,' William continued, walking slowly round the yew.

'Yews are ever so old,' Mary volunteered in a knowledgeable voice. 'We had a project on them at school. Only I wasn't really interested. I think we were told that they're one of our oldest trees. We were supposed to measure the size of the trunks and note where they were growing. They're usually planted in churchyards and other sacred places.'

'Is this a sacred place then?' Alice asked.

'I do think it's strange that everything's in a straight line,' William said, still staring at the tree. 'D'you suppose, if we were in the secret room at Golden House, we could see this tree from the circular window?'

Mary ran back to the edge of the hill, looking down into the valley.

'You'd see the top of it, anyway,' she called.

'Where's Spot?' Alice asked, realizing for the first time that the dog had disappeared. But the other two weren't listening to her. William was walking away towards the standing stone and Mary was squatting on the ground, staring down into Golden Valley.

'Spot,' Alice called. 'Where are you? Spot?'

A quiet yelp drew her attention to the deep

recesses of the yew tree. Its branches spread out in such profusion, reaching out and touching the ground. Now that she looked at it more closely, she realized that it was almost certainly more than one tree. But, however many there were that made up the clump, they grew so closely together that they seemed to form one immense whole.

Again Alice heard Spot yelping. It was a quiet, impatient sound, as though he was calling to her. She walked towards the tree and parted the branches, passing through into the dark interior. It was exactly like going into a room. The ground was quite dry because the thick, interlacing branches formed a roof and walls all around her. At the centre of this room the gnarled and twisted trunks of a number of trees formed a pillar several feet thick. Over the years many of the lower branches had broken or perhaps even been sawn away and where the remaining bits stuck out of the trunks they formed a ladder of most inviting hand and foot holds. Spot was nowhere to be seen, although Alice could still hear him occasionally yelping at a distance. She knew that she should continue to search for him, but the temptation to climb the tree was immense and finally got the better of her. She couldn't resist trying to get to the top. Besides, she argued in her head, I'll be able to get a much better view of everywhere from higher up and I'll probably see Spot and so save a lot of time searching for him down at ground level.

After the first few easy, inviting spurs, she reached the living branches of the tree. At one place she had to work her way round to the other side in order to find a foothold and, later, she reached a place where there were no available branches at all. But here, to her surprise, she found an old iron ring hanging from an iron band that went right round a limb of the tree and, above it, the thickly matted branches pressed in so closely, that she felt she must have reached the top. She was disappointed. She had hoped that she would emerge through the branches and be able to perch, giddily swaying in the breeze, like a bird on a bough. Instead there seemed to be an impenetrable barrier between her and the upper limits of the tree. She reached up and tried to part the thick mass of twigs and branches. But it was difficult because, at the same time, she had to cling on to the iron hoop with her other hand. Then, just as she was about to be defeated, she managed to reach across with one foot and get a firm foothold on another branch. She pulled herself up and round the main trunk at the same time. In front of her a few trimmed pieces of wood had been lodged into a fork in the trunk. They formed a narrow standing place.

Alice stepped across, clinging to a loose branch for support. She was hot and gasping for breath, but elated. Her hands were covered with grime and her jeans were torn where a twig had caught her back pocket as she was pulling herself up. She wiped her brow with the back of her hand and pushed the hair away from her face.

Then she turned and started to edge her way round the main trunk, gripping hold of branches for support and not looking down. When she had almost done a complete circle of the tree she came to a place where a protruding branch made her duck low. Straightening up once more, on the other side of this branch, she found her way blocked. But this time the obstacle took her completely by surprise.

There was a door in the tree.

7
The Magician's Lair

Mary heard Alice's voice calling her name. The sound came from somewhere near to her, but she couldn't see where. She jumped up and ran back round the yew tree, calling:

'William!'

'What?' her brother asked. He was still staring at the standing stone. He looked over his shoulder and saw Mary appear round the side of the big yew.

'Have you seen Alice?'

'She was there a minute ago,' William replied, without showing much interest.

'Well, she's not here now,' Mary told him. 'Oh, bother! She's gone missing again.' Then she heard Alice calling her name again, in an urgent and excited tone. The voice seemed now to be coming from immediately above her head.

'Alice?' she called in a puzzled way, looking up as she did so.

'Oh come quickly,' her sister pleaded. 'I've discovered the most amazing thing.'

'Where are you?' William called, running to join Mary.

'Up in the tree,' Alice called.

'Oh, Alice,' he complained. 'We've stopped playing hide and seek.'

'William Constant, come here at once,' Alice said, sharply. But then her brother and sister heard her gasp, followed by a little 'oh!' of surprise.

'Are you all right?' Mary called, charging through the branches into the depth of the tree, with William following closely behind her.

'Of course she's all right,' a man's voice shouted down at them. 'Now hurry up.'

'Who's that?' William asked, his heart pumping with excitement.

'Where are you?' Mary called, desperately searching the darkness above her. 'Alice? Alice, are you all right?'

But no answer came back.

'Up here, Mare!' William called, as he started to scale the trunk of the tree, using the spurs of wood to reach the upper branches.

Mary followed him, scratching her knee on a protruding twig and scarcely noticing in her haste.

William being taller than Alice found the ascent easier. He soon reached the iron ring and stepped across on to the platform. Then he reached back and took hold of Mary's outstretched hand, helping her across to stand beside him.

'Now where?' Mary whispered. 'Oh, Will! What is going on?'

But William was already edging round the trunk until he reached the low branch.

'Under here, I guess,' he whispered, and he ducked out of her sight. 'Hey!' she heard him exclaim a moment later, from the other side of the branch.

The door in the tree was wide open and Alice was standing on the other side of it, with her back to them. The room she was in was small and many-sided. The walls were made of dark wood and the ceiling rose to a point in the middle, from which was hanging an old iron lantern. All the sides of the room, with the exception of the one with the door in it, were pierced by little pointed windows with no glass in them. Each window had a pointed wooden shutter that opened inwards into the room, with a bolt so that it could be closed securely. At the moment, however, all these shutters were open and daylight filtered into the room through the screen of leaves that surrounded the windows on all sides.

There wasn't any furniture in the room apart from a wooden table and one high backed chair. This chair was at present pulled up to the window immediately opposite to the door and, what is more, it was occupied. Sitting on it, facing the window and with his back consequently turned towards the children, was a man in a long black coat. He was bareheaded and his thin hair surrounded his head like a red mist.

'It's Mr Tyler!' Mary gasped.

'Sssh!' the man said, without looking round. Then he raised to his eyes a pair of binoculars, which had been resting on his lap, and peered through them.

'Interesting!' he muttered. 'But what is it for?'

'You're holding it the wrong way round,' William advised him, sounding more than a little nervous at his own presumption.

'Wrong way?' the man said, his voice stern.

'Does this thing belong to you?' and, as he spoke, he turned in his chair and for the first time the three children could see his face.

'Oh, Mr Tyler,' Alice cried. 'I'm ever so pleased you've come. I've been longing to . . . '

'Silence!' Stephen Tyler thundered.

Alice gulped.

' . . . longing to ask you all sorts of questions,' she determinedly finished her sentence, but in a voice that grew quieter and quieter until it ended in a whisper.

'To whom does this thing belong?' Stephen Tyler demanded, waving the binoculars in front of him.

The three children shrugged but were too nervous to actually speak. The man seemed in a bad temper, which was off putting, but, more than that, now that they were once more standing in front of him, and in spite of their delight at seeing him again, they felt shy and uncertain.

Stephen Tyler sighed, irritably.

'Oh, come on! I haven't got all day,' he said, then he added, in a tone that betrayed a certain reluctance to admit his own ignorance: 'Wrong way round, do you say?' And, turning once more to look out of the window, he raised the binoculars to his eyes in the correct position and gasped with pleasure. 'Oh, that's splendid!' he cried. 'I couldn't see any sense in an instrument that made the distance seem further away . . . But to bring it nearer to one is an altogether different matter. I say, how very clever.'

'But haven't you seen a telescope before?' William asked.

'Telescope?' the man muttered.

'The telescope was invented by Galileo,' Mary chimed in, using her smug, I-know-because-I'm-good-at-history voice.

'Galileo?' Stephen Tyler said, swinging round once more and fixing her with his piercingly blue eyes. 'You know this man?'

'No!' Mary snorted, as though she was about to laugh and then managed to stop herself just in time. 'I mean, I learned about him in history.'

'History?' Stephen Tyler said, thoughtfully, then shook his head. 'Oh, yes, of course. I keep forgetting. I am history to you and you are the future to me. It is all most. . . . Who is this Galileo?'

'Well,' Mary answered, stuffing her hands into her jeans pockets and staring at her feet, trying to remember anything at all about him. 'He invented the telescope.' Then she hesitated. The man was staring at her so fiercely, that he made her unsure of her facts. 'At least, I think he did,' she mumbled.

'Telescope? What is this telescope that I keep hearing you mention?'

'It's another instrument for looking into the distance,' William joined in. 'Only it's much more powerful and there's only one hole to look through. . . . Oooh, it's very difficult explaining these things.'

'Yes, isn't it?' Stephen Tyler agreed, staring at William now.

'A telescope is used for looking at the stars,' William started again, trying to sound confident while feeling acutely nervous.

'Looking at the stars?' Stephen Tyler sighed.

He sounded almost sad. 'How I wish I'd been born later. There is so much knowledge that I lack.'

'But, I don't think there's been anyone, ever, anywhere, apart from you who can time travel,' Alice told him, filled with admiration and not wanting him to be sad.

'No, no. You misunderstand me, little girl,' the Magician told her. 'I know I'm brilliant, it's just that I lack the insight of later discovery and knowledge. The stars are a great mystery. I would have liked to probe them before I die . . . ' Then, changing the subject abruptly, he swung round to stare at them once more. 'Who has been using this tree room?' he demanded.

'We don't know,' Alice replied with a shrug. 'We've only just found it ourselves.'

'But surely you didn't find this place on your own, did you?' Stephen Tyler asked.

'Well, not exactly, no. Spot sort of drew my attention to it,' Alice admitted.

'Spot?'

'The dog,' Mary reminded him.

'Ah, yes. The dog. Well, good, good. I wouldn't want this place to be too obvious,' the Magician told them. 'Right, now, to work. How has it all been going since I last saw you? When was that, I wonder? Yesterday?'

'Three months ago,' Mary told him. 'We've had a whole term at school since we were last here.'

'Oh, yes. School!' the Magician said in a withering voice. 'Totally useless institutions, in my opinion. They teach none of the right subjects.'

'Well, we are taught chemistry and science now,' William told him.

65

'Chimistrie?' Stephen Tyler thundered. 'They teach children chimistrie? Most unsuitable.'

'Well what should they teach us then?' Alice demanded.

'They should teach little girls not to ask questions all the time and they should teach little boys not to know all the answers,' he snapped. And then, quite unexpectedly, he laughed aloud and clapped his hands. 'Splendid, splendid. How good that we're all together again. I can't stay long this time. I only came up here to check on the . . . ' he frowned and shook his head. 'What was I going to check? It really is most essential that you learn everything there is to learn before you become old. Because then, you will find that the mind lets you down. That, to a magician, is a most tiresome experience. What was I saying . . . ? Oh, yes. How long will you be staying at Gelden House?'

'Just over a week,' Mary told him.

'Is that all?' the man asked. 'But there is so much to be done. Never mind. At least you've started. How did you like the first lesson?'

The three children blinked. They hadn't an inkling what he was talking about.

'What lesson?' Alice asked.

'Well, what are you here for?' Stephen Tyler sounded cross again and then immediately seemed to relent and softened his tone. 'I'll tell you, shall I? Would that be best?'

Alice nodded, emphatically. She was not at all keen on being lectured to but she was even less fond of being snapped at and, what was more, she was in danger of saying so, Magician or no Magician.

'Before you return to your places of learning,

66

I want you to understand the . . . world of the natural.'

'The natural?' William demanded, 'What's that?'

'Nature,' Stephen Tyler snapped. 'You must have heard of nature?'

'Yes, of course,' William mumbled. 'I just didn't understand . . . '

'No, of course you wouldn't,' the old man said, more kindly. 'The last thing they teach you in a school is any of this,' and he gestured out of the window at the bright world beyond. 'But it is essential, for our work, that you three come to understand the world of the animals and of the birds.'

'For our work?' Mary asked, eagerly. 'What is our work, Mr Tyler?'

The Magician looked at her closely.

'A good question,' he said. 'Our work is on ourselves. We each have to discover ourselves – or rather our self; our true Self. And then we must discover our place in the order of things. Finally, we will, each of us, have to do our duty.'

'Oh,' William groaned, 'it's not like belonging to the scouts, is it?'

'Scouts?' Stephen Tyler asked.

'Doesn't matter,' Williiam said.

'William hated the scouts,' Alice whispered confidentially. 'He thought it was silly.'

'I promise you, our work is not silly,' the Magician assured them.

'So, what you mean is . . . ' Mary said, frowning and trying hard to follow what was being said, ' . . . we have to be good at botany and biology and stuff?'

'No, no. Listen to me,' the Magician said, holding up his hand. 'It really is much more simple than we allow it to be. Man – you and me, all of us – Man is a part of the natural world, but Man has become separated from his origins . . . '

'You mean we're really animals?' William asked, with a flash of understanding.

'Yes!' Stephen Tyler cried. 'But most tricksy animals! The Human Being has the potential to be an angel and the aptitude to be a beast. It is vital to be able to separate the chaff from the wheat, the dross from the gold, the impure from the pure. But you have to discover this aptitude for yourselves. It is an important part of the work. Let me know how you get on.'

'Has all this something to do with Alchemy?' William asked.

'Certainly,' the Magician replied. 'It has everything to do with it. But don't try to walk before you can even crawl. That's what Morden, my assistant, is doing – with the most regrettable results.' Then he lowered his voice and leaned towards them. 'It isn't really safe meeting in the upper chamber any more. Morden is always listening. And besides, in your own time, someone seems to have discovered its whereabouts.'

William gasped.

'You mean somebody else knows about the secret room as well as us?'

'I do. Yes.'

'Are you sure? But who?'

'I am certain. But I don't know who it is,' the man replied. 'I can always tell when someone has been in. I'm expecting you to discover who it is . . . '

Then suddenly, in mid sentence, he sat bolt upright on his chair, and turned his head to the side, darting it forward like a bird and listening intently.

'There's someone coming up the tree,' he whispered.

The children hadn't heard a sound. But the Magician raised a finger to his lips and then pointed towards the open door. As they turned and looked out of the room, they could see the narrow landing outside and the branch blocking the way.

The light beyond the door was poor. As they watched they saw a foot appear below the branch. It was wearing a very muddy wellington boot. Then a hand appeared under the branch, feeling its way and the hand was followed by an arm and the arm by a shoulder and the top of a head. It was like watching a human figure materialising before their eyes. The head was covered by an old and battered trilby hat. The figure, as it rose upright, having negotiated the branch, was seen to be dressed in a brown mac, belted at the waist with a piece of string. The person was short and stocky. The wellingtons reached to the hem of the mac. The light was too dim to get a clear impression of the face.

'Well, now!' a woman's voice exclaimed. 'Who are all of you, I wonder? And what are you doing in my hidey hole?'

Mary stepped forward, not because she was the bravest, but because she was nearest the door and there wasn't much room for the others to pass her.

'We're not doing any harm,' she said. 'Honestly.'

'Bless you, I didn't think you would be,' the woman told her as she walked into the room.

Now that she was standing in the light that came in through all the windows, they were able to see her better. She had a round, rosy-cheeked face with a shock of wild white hair sticking out from under the man's hat she was wearing. Her mac was bunched round her waist and her wellingtons were caked with mud. She looked not unlike a cheerful scarecrow. Her eyes twinkled and her smile revealed irregular, but very white, teeth.

'Children?' she said. 'What are children doing in my hidey hole. And, God love us! A kestrel at the window!' and she reached out with a gnarled hand to where a moment before Stephen Tyler had been sitting in the chair. The children turned quickly and saw a sleek grey and brown bird, perched on the sill of the window, staring over its shoulder at them.

'Well, Kes!' the woman said, softly. 'You're not one that I recognize. I should have brought a mouse for you, if I'd known. Come, Kes,' she whispered, holding out the back of her hand.

But the bird refused to be drawn and remained aloof and staring.

'You have to be a bit careful with them. A kestrel can give you a savage nip and those claws could tear your hand off. What d'you call it then?' the woman said, looking at the children.

'Kee Kee,' Alice replied on an impulse.

'There now, Kee Kee,' the woman said, reaching out once more to the bird. 'Can't we be friends?'

But the bird only cocked its head on one side and blinked at her. Then, turning, it launched itself

70

off the sill and out through the branches into the dazzling light beyond.

'Kee! Kee! Kee!' they heard it cry as it flew out of their sight.

'Now there's a strange thing,' the woman said, leaning on the sill, with her back to the children, as she followed the bird's flight. Then she turned back into the room and smiled at them once more. 'Here we all are,' she said, 'not knowing who we are and the only one with a name has left us.' And she laughed, a light, chuckling sound. 'I'm Meg Lewis,' she told them. 'And who might you all be?'

As the children introduced themselves, the kestrel's distant, mournful, cry could be heard again as he flew somewhere, up above them, beyond the pointed roof and the matted branches of the tree, in the clear blue sky.

'Kee! Kee! Kee!' he called, as if he were saying goodbye.

8
Meg Lewis Tells Her Story

For a moment there was silence in the little tree house. The woman who had called herself Meg Lewis looked at the children and they, in turn, looked at her.

'Silence reigned, and we all got wet!' Meg said eventually. 'Cat got your tongues?'

'We didn't mean to trespass,' William said.

'No,' Meg nodded. 'No more you did. Tell you the truth, I'm not sure that I can claim this place as my own, anyway. Let's just say that I make use of it. So, who's to say I don't trespass myself? But I doubt the true owner minds or even knows, for I think he or she must have gone many years ago. I found this place quite by chance one night, when I was on the watch. It came on to rain, you see, and I stepped under the spreading branches of the tree to shelter. Well, one thing lead to another, didn't it? Just as it happened for you, I expect, and I found my way up here. Mind, I've done a bit of repairing. It's been here for a good while, I reckon. That lantern is a fair age – and the wood these walls are made of is solid oak. Oak! There's not

72

much building done with oak these days, now is there? But I had thought I was the only one who knew of this room, and here you all are. You're not from these parts, are you?'

'No,' Mary said. 'We're staying with our uncle.'

'And who might he be?' Meg asked her.

'His name is Jack Green. He lives in Golden House. It's the big house down in the valley over there . . . ' Mary explained, pointing as she did so out of the window, where the chimneys of the house could just be seen rising above the trees, down at the bottom of the almost sheer drop.

'Yes, I know Golden House,' Meg said. 'Time was my family lived there. But that was a while ago now, wasn't it? Before we hit bad times. And now the Lewis family don't live there any more and it's the Greens, is it? Ah, that's what I came back for!' she exclaimed, picking up the binoculars from where they lay on the seat of the chair. 'My prize possession. Given to me by a policeman. What d'you think of that, then?'

'D'you come here to bird watch?' William asked her, feeling less nervous now. He decided he liked Meg, even if she did look a bit wild and had a funny way of dressing.

'God love you! What time have I got to bird watch?' Meg exclaimed. 'I've two cows and six sheep. Four fields to tend. Water to draw from the well. Lamps to trim. A fire to lay. The dogs and the cats. The rabbits, which are a blimmin nuisance, though I say it who shouldn't. And a rascal of a squirrel that leads me a dance. And all that just during the hours of daylight. The nights are when I do most of my work.'

'What work?' Mary asked.

Meg turned and looked out through one of the windows.

'I can't rightly call it work, I suppose. Not real work like most people do. But it's work to me. Not hardship, I mean. Never that. A privilege.' She fell silent, staring out into the distance.

'But, what do you do?' Alice asked her.

'I go about the woodlands, keeping watch.'

'For what?'

'For the men who come with the torches,' Meg replied.

'What do they do with their torches?' William asked her, puzzled.

'You're too young to bother with these things,' Meg said, looking back at them. Then she frowned and turned away again, speaking almost to herself. 'We've been free of it here in Golden Valley for a good while now. But it's happening again.'

'That's what Spot said,' Alice whispered to Mary and William. 'Don't you remember? When we found the dead badger.'

Meg swung round, a look of shock on her face.

'What did you say?' she asked.

'It was yesterday . . . You see, I got lost in the forest and Spot came to find me . . . '

'A dead badger, did you say?' Meg gasped. 'How dead?'

'Very,' Alice answered. 'Uncle Jack helped us bury it just now.'

'Poor beast,' Meg sighed. 'That was good of you to bury it. I wonder which one it was.'

'Spot called it Brock,' William volunteered eagerly.

'Brock? Not Brock,' Meg's voice was full of sadness. 'How did you know this?' Who is this . . . Spot did you say?'

'He's our dog,' Alice explained. 'At least, he lives at Golden House. Well, he does now. He came from . . . I don't really know where he came from, exactly. But he's our dog now. Anyway, he led us to a place called the Dark and Something Path . . . '

'The Dark and Dreadful Path,' Meg said, quietly. 'You've been there?'

'Yes,' Alice whispered. 'Why is it called that?'

'If you've been there, then surely you don't need to ask, do you?'

Alice shook her head and shuffled her feet. She didn't really understand the answer, but felt she should and so remained silent.

'This dog of yours,' Meg continued. 'He's an unusual creature. It seems he talks to you and you understand him.'

'Oh, yes,' Alice agreed, enthusiastically. 'He's the Magician's dog really . . . '

The words were out before she could stop herself. She knew at once what a stupid thing she'd done. She could feel the blood rushing to her cheeks and William and Mary were looking at her with such dismay. But the reaction of Meg Lewis was strangest of all. She dropped the binoculars back on the chair seat and raised her hands to cover her ears as though she was trying to avoid a terrible sound.

'Magician?' she whispered. Then she looked

quickly round the room, as though she half expected Stephen Tyler suddenly to appear.

William who had watched her closely from the start now frowned.

'You know about the Magician?' he asked her, in a half whisper.

'I know nothing,' Meg replied, 'and I wonder how you do. But, of course, you come from that house. That would explain a lot.' She turned, quickly, closing all the shutters one by one with a bang so that the light in the room was gradually reduced until they were standing in darkness. Then she crossed to the door. 'I'd like to meet this dog of yours,' she said as she went out on to the landing. 'Last one out close the door after them,' and she ducked out of sight beneath the hanging branch.

'Alice,' William groaned.

'I'm sorry,' she whispered. 'It just slipped out.'

'We were never to mention the Magician to anyone.'

'I'm sorry, Will. Honestly I am.'

'She didn't do it on purpose, Will,' Mary said. 'And anyway, I think Meg Lewis had heard of the Magician before. You saw how she reacted when Alice mentioned him. It was like as if she was scared or something.'

'Oh, frog's legs!' Alice exclaimed. 'You don't suppose she's an enemy? Someone belonging to that assistant of Mr Tyler's, do you?'

'Like the rat was, you mean?' Mary said. 'What d'you think, Will?'

'I don't know,' William answered. 'I can't believe she is. I mean she seems nice. The rat wasn't nice at all.'

'No, he wasn't.' Alice agreed with a shudder, remembering the rat that had so terrified her at Christmas.

'Come on,' William said. 'We'd better go down. She'll be waiting for us.'

When they emerged out of the branches of the tree, Meg was standing on the grass, in the bright sunlight, with Spot sitting at her feet. His tail was wagging and he was looking up at her, as though he expected her to give him a treat.

'Spot!' Alice exclaimed, taken completely by surprise.

'So, this is your Spot,' Meg said, stroking the dog's head. 'Well, Spot,' she said gently to the dog, 'you've had other names in your time, haven't you? I used to call him Gypsy – for he was ever a wanderer. And my father had a dog just like him that he called Blackbane.'

At the sound of this last name, Spot whined and cowered away from Meg, with his tail between his legs. Alice ran forward, putting an arm round the dog's shoulder, as if protecting him.

'There, child,' Meg said, gently, 'I wouldn't harm him. It's my words he doesn't like. Blackbane and my father fell out.' She shook her head and frowned. 'I never knew the half of what went on. But I promise you, I'm the animals' friend. You ask your Spot. I must get home.' She looked up at the sky again. 'The nights will be long again for a while.' And she turned and walked away from them towards the standing stone.

'Miss Lewis,' William called, running after her.

'Bless you, boy! Call me Meg, everyone else does,' Meg said, stopping and turning to him.

'Please tell us what all this is about,' he said. 'The dead badger and the Dark and Dreadful Path. We might be able to do something. We're only here for a bit but. . . . We would like to help.'

'Help?' Meg asked, frowning. Why?'

'I don't know, really,' William mumbled. 'It's just . . . we want to understand about the country and everything and . . . '

'Badger baiting,' Meg cut in.

'Sorry?' William asked, not fully understanding what she had said.

'Around here is one of the finest badger setts in our country. The badgers are my friends. All animals are, really. I prefer animals to people. But the badgers are special. And the foxes. The poor foxes. There is a hunt here, every winter. I won't let them across my land. I'm despised for that.'

'Do you know where the foxes live?' William asked, remembering Cinnabar.

'You like the foxes?' Meg asked him. 'Yes, I could take you. But now my work will be cut out. Men come, out from the towns mostly. They have snappy little terrier dogs and some of them have lurchers and pit bulls . . . hard dogs, not like animals, vicious like their masters. They come at night, with torches. They send the dogs down the setts to flush the badgers out. They put nets over the holes, then when a badger comes out, they catch it. Or, sometimes, they just stun the poor beast with the back of a shovel, and take him that way.'

'But, why?' Alice asked. 'What for?'

'Sport,' Meg replied.

'Sport?' William exclaimed. 'How can that be sport?'

'They set their dogs against the badgers. Sometimes the dogs are badly mauled. They bet on their dogs; put money on which one will beat the badger.'

'Beat?' Mary asked, horrified.

'Conquer, beat, defeat, kill,' Meg said the words slowly, sadly almost.

'But, that's horrible,' Mary said, her voice shaking. 'That's not sport. D'you suppose that's what happened to the one we saw?'

'Almost certainly,' Meg replied.

'But what can you do about it, Meg?' William asked.

'It's against the law – so, if I catch them at it, I report them to the police. I get photographs of them, with my flash. I note the numberplates of their cars. I follow them.' She walked away from the children, thoughtfully, until she was level with the standing stone, then she turned. 'What puzzles me though is that we've been quiet for a while. I thought the men had all given up. There was quite a roundup by the police last year. Heavy fines were imposed. I thought we'd seen the last of them. Where have this new lot come from? That's what I don't know.' She looked up at the sun, hanging low over the top of the trees. 'I must go back, soon be evening.' And, with a wave of the hand, she turned and walked away from them.

'Come and see me at Four Fields,' she called, without looking back.

9
Phoebe Reads the Riot Act

It was the middle of the afternoon, far later than they had realized. They ran down the steep hillside, dodging in and out of the trees, following Spot, who raced ahead of them, his tail streaming out behind and his ears flapping.

Alice was soon lagging behind and had to call out to them to wait for her.

'I have got the shortest legs, you know. It's OK for you two,' she protested, as she slithered and scrambled down towards them.

The route they took was in an almost straight line from the yew. The tree house was completely hidden by the green branches.

'And, of course,' William said, looking back up the steep gradient, as they waited for Alice, 'yew is evergreen. So that means the room must be secret, summer and winter.'

No sooner did Alice catch up, than, ahead of them, Spot barked impatiently, urging them on.

'It isn't fair,' she yelled, as the other two immediately ran ahead again. 'I didn't get to have any rest. Oh, frogspawn!' she swore violently, to no one in particular, and, feeling better, she set off in pursuit once more.

The ground became ever more steep. They had to hang on to the trunks of the trees to prevent themselves falling. They skirted an outcrop of rock. They pushed their way through vast clumps of undergrowth, with vicious brambles and long branches of briar rose. They slipped and slid between the roots of chestnut trees and through thick coverts of broom and gorse. They panted and gasped and sometimes they tripped and tumbled as they followed Spot's dizzying career down towards the valley bottom.

Alice thought her lungs would burst for want of breath and Mary, who was in the lead, dug her knuckles into the side of her waist to fight off the pain of a stitch. Eventually they reached the same forest track that they'd started out from. Here William collapsed in a heap on the grassy verge, and lay back, sweating and fighting for breath.

'Oh!' he sobbed. 'I can't go another step.'

But Spot was already chasing off along the track. They had arrived at a point some distance from the gate into the kitchen garden and in the opposite direction to the way they had taken when leaving the house that morning.

'You can't see any path at all,' Mary said, staring back up the wooded hillside and searching the distant tree line for any sign of the yew tree house.

'I've been cut to ribbons on those thorns,' Alice complained, rubbing a long thin scratch on one of her arms.

Then, ahead of them, they heard Spot barking

impatiently again. So they hurried to follow him, Alice and Mary dragging William up on to his feet while he continued to protest that he couldn't move another inch.

'Honestly, Will!' Alice mocked him, 'you are hopeless! Don't you do any exercise at that school of yours?' Then she dodged away from him and ran ahead, screaming and laughing, with William chasing after her.

They found Spot standing outside the wooden gate set into the high brick wall that led into the kitchen garden. The gate was closed and so he was unable to enter. But the moment Alice pushed it open, he shot past her, almost knocking her over in his impatience to be inside.

'What is the matter with him?' Alice complained, irritably.

The dog streaked down the length of the garden and out through the gate into the yard without waiting for them.

'Maybe it's his dinner time,' Mary suggested.

'I must admit I'm starving,' Alice agreed.

But, as they approached the yard gate, their steps got slower and slower.

'We're so late. What are we going to say?' William said, voicing all their thoughts.

'We'll just have to tell the truth,' Alice said. 'Say we didn't realize how late it was and explain what happened.'

'But we can't say what we've been doing,' William protested, 'without mentioning the Magician.'

'Maybe we could say that we got lost again,' Mary suggested.

'But we didn't,' William said. 'And I wasn't even really lost yesterday. Not really.'

'Well, I certainly was,' Alice said. 'I went round and round in circles in that foul forest. If it hadn't been for Spot, I expect I'd have faded away and died in there.'

'And the kestrel,' Mary added. 'It was the kestrel who showed us where you were.' Then she shuddered. 'It was a vile place, wasn't it? I don't think I shall go back there again.'

'Maybe we'll have to,' William said. 'Maybe that's what Mr Tyler meant about learning about the natural world.'

'Well, I won't go back in that pine forest, not ever. Not for anyone,' Alice declared. 'I wouldn't go near that Dark and Dreadful Path again – not even for the Magician.' And, as she finished speaking, far above them in the pale sky a kestrel wheeled and cried:

'Kee! Kee! Kee!'

'Oh,' Alice whispered, looking up. 'D'you suppose he heard me?' and she hurried forward towards the yard gate.

Phoebe was standing at the kitchen door, with Spot beside her. She was drying her hands on a towel and when she saw the children she threw the towel down on the doorstep and came quickly towards them.

'Where on earth have you been?' she cried. 'Jack's been searching everywhere for you.'

'Sorry, Phoebe,' Mary said. 'We didn't realize how late it was.'

'You've been gone for hours,' Phoebe shouted. She was in a terrible temper and for a moment it almost looked as if she was going to hit one of them. Her fists were clenched and she banged them against her thighs, her anger making her movements tense and her voice shrill.

'We really are sorry,' William said. 'We sort of went further than we meant and . . . we . . . well, we . . . '

' . . . didn't realize how late it was,' Alice cut in, sounding a bit fed up with the need to explain. 'Sorry!'

'Sorry?' Phoebe exclaimed. 'You're sorry? Have you any idea what I've been going through? You're here in our charge and you disappear for most of the day. I couldn't believe it when Jack said he'd let you go off again. Come in, at once. There was a lunch waiting for you. I've had to throw most of it away.'

She turned her back on them and walked into the kitchen, picking up the towel from the doorstep.

Alice pulled a long face and shrugged.

'Oh, fishcakes!' she whispered. 'She's throwing a real wobbly.'

'Come on,' William told them, in a resigned tone.

'I bet she didn't need to throw the food away. She just said that to make us feel worse.'

'She's right, though,' William said. 'We have been away hours, it's no wonder she was worried.'

'We shall just have to tell her the truth,' Mary said, following him across the yard.

'What truth?' William asked, obviously surprised.

'Everything that happened,' Mary replied.

'What? Even about the Magician?' Alice asked.

84

'Why not?' Mary asked. 'He contributed to us being late. If we hadn't seen him, we'd have left the tree house much sooner and we'd have missed Meg and we'd have been home ages ago. Well, a bit earlier, anyway.'

'We can't tell Phoebe about the Magician, Mary,' William told her. 'She wouldn't believe us.'

'She might. It'd be worth finding out. Besides, it isn't our fault if we tell the truth and then we aren't believed, is it?'

Phoebe appeared at the door again and shouted, angrily:

'I said come in. Now, this minute. Do as you're told.'

Spot was sitting near the kitchen range. He looked up, as the children entered, and whined.

'And I'm disappointed with you as well, Spot,' Phoebe snapped, crossing to the sink. 'You were supposed to be looking after them.'

'But he did!' Alice cried out in dismay. 'We'd never have found our way if it hadn't been for Spot.'

'Be quiet, Alice,' Phoebe said, swinging round and glaring at her.

'No, Phoebe,' Alice bravely insisted, running across and putting a protective arm round the dog, who trembled and whined miserably. 'Blame us as much as you like, but please don't be cross with Spot. He didn't do anything wrong. Punish me if you want to. But please not Spot.' She finished speaking in a tiny, trembling voice and she swallowed hard and blinked, trying to clear the tears that had suddenly filled her eyes.

Spot pushed close to her and turned his head to give her cheek a brief, surreptitious lick. This was too much for Alice, who buried her face on the dog's shoulder and howled noisily.

The sound of Alice woke Stephanie, who had been sleeping in her cot at the other side of the kitchen range. She started to cry on a high pitched note and then Spot, hearing the baby's distress and bearing the weight of Alice round his neck, added to the din by raising his head and baying mournfully.

The hall door opened and Jack came into the room.

'What the hell is going on in here?' he yelled. 'Shut up, all of you. You, Spot. . . . Be quiet . . . '

But his shouting only added to the commotion, as the dog, the baby and Alice each continued to grieve with renewed vigour.

'Stop it!' Jack yelled, covering his ears with his hands. Phoebe crossed, picked up the baby and, rocking her in her arms to soothe her, hurried from the room.

Jack, meanwhile, pulled Alice away from Spot and put his arms round her.

'What is the matter with you, child?' he yelled, as she continued to sob in front of him.

Spot crawled away towards his basket, by the back door, and curled up in it, his eyes open, watching every movement in the room.

All this time Mary and William had remained standing half way across the kitchen between the door and the range, which was where they'd arrived when Alice had first started to bawl.

'Can't you do something to stop her, Mary?' Jack shouted as Alice continued to sob noisily.

Mary simply shook her head and remained silent. She'd seen it all before.

'She'll stop in a minute if you ignore her,' William said.

'How can you ignore a noise like this?' Jack demanded. 'It's worse than a cat in a rain storm!' And he mewed tragically, putting his face close to Alice and shaking his head.

Alice was half way through a new howl but, seeing Jack's cat impersonation, she gulped and smiled.

'That's better,' he said, gently. Then he wiped the tears off her cheeks with his hands and put an arm round her shoulders. 'All right, you lot. You've got some explaining to do.' He raised a finger. 'But not to me,' he added, 'to Phoebe,' and he pointed towards the hall door, through which Phoebe had departed. 'She's been worried sick about you. You'd better have a good story ready. You were supposed to be back for lunch. She's going to read you the riot act – and I wouldn't be in any of your shoes while she does it. There's nothing more terrifying than Phoebe when she's in a temper.'

Spot grunted and closed his eyes, obviously hoping to avoid the wrath to come by sleeping.

'It honestly was a mistake, Uncle Jack,' Mary said.

'Don't tell me,' Jack protested. 'Tell her,' and, as he spoke, Phoebe came back into the room.

'She's quiet now,' she said, obviously referring to Stephanie, whom she had left in some other part of the house. 'Go on, Spot,' she continued as she walked over to the kitchen range, 'go and sit with Steph.'

Spot rose quickly and scampered away into the hall, relieved to be out of the room. Phoebe, meanwhile, put some logs on the range fire and raked out the hot ashes with a poker.

There was an awkward silence in the room. Alice sidled across to stand between William and Mary. She felt vulnerable standing on her own, Uncle Jack having followed Phoebe to the fire as soon as she entered. He now put his hands on either side of Phoebe's waist and turned her so that she was looking at him.

'All right?' he asked her gently.

The children saw Phoebe frown slightly, then she passed the back of a hand across her forehead, brushing some stray hairs away from her eyes.

'Don't Jack, please,' she said, pushing him away gently but firmly. 'Well, where've you been?' she asked the children, turning to look at them.

'We met a woman called Meg Lewis,' Mary told her. Then, when this brought no response from Phoebe, she shrugged and continued. 'I think she lives somewhere near here. Anyway she knew this house. She said her family used to live here . . . '

'Jonas Lewis,' Phoebe said quietly. 'Don't you remember, Jack? That book you borrowed from the woman at the museum, when the children were here at Christmas.'

'Of course!' William exclaimed. 'The book about alchemy. Have you still got it, Uncle Jack?'

'No. I returned it to Miss Prewett. Apparently the man she'd borrowed it from decided to give it to the museum . . . '

'As far as I can remember,' William continued, thinking out loud, 'Jonas Lewis left Golden House right at the end of the last century. D'you think he could have been Meg's father?'

'How old is she?' Jack asked, his curiosity aroused.

Mary shrugged.

'Probably older than she looks. She has a sort of unlined face, you know? One of those pale, shiny faces, that always look as if they've just been washed. But her hair's all white. It's difficult to tell what age she is. I mean she wasn't too old to climb a tree . . . '

'Climb a tree?' Jack asked, with a laugh. 'I think you'd better begin at the beginning!'

And so the children started to recount the events of the day, all talking at once and adding bits that the others had left out. But not one of them mentioned seeing Stephen Tyler. Mary later said that she'd fully intended to, but that, when it came to it, she'd realized that Jack wouldn't begin to understand or believe her, and she didn't want to stop the conversation, which had been going rather well.

Jack questioned them closely about the tree house and was obviously delighted by the sound of it.

'You must take me and show me,' he said.

Then they'd gone on to tell him about Meg's arrival and about the badger baiters.

'Here? In our valley?' Jack asked. 'I'm sure that can't be true. I'd know if there were people wandering about here . . . '

'But not in the middle of the night, Uncle Jack,' William had pointed out.

All the time they were talking. Phoebe stood near the hearth, half turned away from them, as though she was scarcely listening. But, when Jack said that he'd pop in and see Miss Prewett the next time he was in town and ask her if he could borrow the Jonas Lewis book again, she suddenly rounded on them.

'No!' she said, vehemently. 'No, Jack. Listen to you. You promised me that we'd leave all this alone. I want nothing more to do with it.'

She paced away from them, as the children watched her silently, then turned once more. They saw that she had a wild, desperate look. 'There are too many unexplained things; too many strange events; too many noises. I wish we'd never come here. What possessed us to move to this great big, crumbling house . . . ? It needs a fortune spending on it and it's already taking what little money we've got saved just to prop it up.'

'Well, it was mainly your idea, darling,' Jack put in, mildly. Then he glanced at the children, obviously not wanting to have this conversation in front of them.

'Yes, all right,' Phoebe replied. 'I know that. I admit it. So, I was wrong. When we came and saw the place, I felt as though I was coming home. Home!' she laughed, a sad, dry, brittle sound. 'I hate it here,' she sobbed. 'It gets hold of you. Already I hardly see you, Jack. You're all the time working on the house . . . '

'I'll get the builders back,' Jack cut in.

'The builders?' Phoebe cried. 'This place is costing us a fortune. Oh, what's the use . . . ' she sighed, and she crossed quickly to the door. 'For as long as you're here, children, I don't want you disappearing off into the forest without telling me where you're going. I can't stand any more worry, you hear me? I've had enough . . . ' and she fled from the room, banging the door shut after her.

The children looked at the floor. It was horribly embarrassing and none of them knew exactly what to do or say.

'Oh, dear!' Jack sighed. 'Sorry about that.'

'It's our fault,' Mary told him. 'It was wrong of us to be out so long.'

'It's not just that,' Jack said, shaking his head. 'It's all been getting her down a bit. She gets really worried about money. Maybe I should get that book back from Miss Prewett and see if I can't do a bit of alchemy myself! I could do with a few gold bars!'

'No, Uncle Jack!' William cried, earnestly.

'I was only joking, William!' Jack said. 'Don't tell me you believe in all that rubbish? You'll have to join up with Phoebe. She's convinced this place is full of magic and I don't know what other nonsense.' He crossed to the door. 'I'll just go and . . . try and cheer her up, I suppose. I won't be a minute,' and he hurried from the room.

'Chocolate cupcakes!' Alice exclaimed, when they were alone. 'Was that the riot act?'

William whistled and shook his hand as though he'd just burnt it.

'Oh, William,' Mary said, 'you don't think Uncle Jack was serious about using the alchemy to make himself some gold?'

'No! I'm sure he wasn't. I mean – he said himself, he thinks it's all a load of nonsense.'

'All the same,' Mary continued, deep in thought, 'they've obviously come across something.'

'Mr Tyler said that other people had discovered the secret room,' Alice whispered. 'D'you suppose it was Phoebe and Jack and they're not letting us know? Ooh the liars!'

'We'd better go up there as soon as we get the chance,' William declared. 'There are a lot of things we have to find out.'

10
The Writing on the Mirror

It was a very subdued supper. Jack tried making cheerful conversation, but that only seemed to make matters worse. Nobody was in the mood to talk and what few jokes he attemped fell flat. Phoebe clearly regretted her earlier behaviour but, at the same time, was still cross with the children – probably because they had caused her to lose her temper in the first place. She hardly spoke at all, and when she did it was only to offer second helpings or to ask Jack to bring something to the table. Spot remained curled up in his basket as if he'd decided the wisest thing was to keep his head down and, for the most part, even Stephanie lay quietly sleeping in her cot.

The children were tired after all the exertions of the day. Although they were hungry, they scarcely had the energy or the desire to eat. The backs of their legs ached, all their individual cuts and scratches smarted and they felt embarrassed and uncomfortable in that edgy, oppressive atmosphere that always follows a row.

Towards the end of the meal Stephanie woke and started to cry fretfully. So, as soon as she'd finished eating, Phoebe lifted her from the cot and nursed her, sitting on a chair by the fire. Then, when she couldn't get the baby to settle, she loosened the top of her dress and bared one of her breasts. After a moment the baby started to suck.

Alice watched this whole procedure with such open-mouthed disbelief that Mary had to kick her under the table. William could feel his cheeks getting scarlet with embarrassment and even Mary wasn't quite sure where to look and ended up studying the back of her hand with intense interest. The only person who seemed not in the least perturbed was Jack who continued to eat his food as though nothing out-of-the-ordinary was happening.

As soon as supper was finished, Jack and Alice cleared the table and Mary and William started to wash up. The children couldn't get the job done fast enough and, as soon as the last dish was dried and put away, Mary suggested going to bed. They said hurried goodnights to Jack and Phoebe, avoiding, as much as possible, looking at the naked breast and the contented baby that lay sucking in Phoebe's arms. Then they escaped from the kitchen and went up to the girl's room.

'Sausages!' Alice groaned, sinking down on to the floor in front of the electric fire. 'Wasn't that awful? I just wanted to disappear. When she got her boob out! What did she think she was doing?'

'Feeding Stephanie, Alice!' Mary told her, in a superior tone.

'I know that, Mary,' Alice answered her back. 'I'm not entirely stupid, you know. But to just sit there . . . doing it! Ugh! I mean . . . I just happen to think it was the rudest thing I've ever seen.'

'It wasn't really,' Mary said. 'It's quite natural.'

'But – not while we're eating, Mary!' William protested.

'Well, that's decided me,' Alice said. 'I'm never going to have a baby. Not ever. The thought of it makes me feel all. . . . Ugh!' she shuddered and shook her head. 'Besides, I refuse to have breasts. I think they're hideous!'

'Oh, shut up, Alice!'

'You're blushing, William!' Mary giggled.

'William! You are!' Alice exclaimed. Then she also started to giggle.

'Don't you like talking about women's breasts, William?' Mary goaded him. 'D'you think there's something a bit . . . sexy about them?' and she giggled again.

Then Alice jumped up and threw herself at him, chanting: 'Boobs! Boobs! Will's got a thing about boobs!'

'Get off!' William yelled, and pushing her away he made a dash for the door. 'I'm going to bed.'

'But – when are we going up to the secret room?' Alice asked.

'In the morning, before the others are up. I'll set the alarm for six,' he replied, going across the landing to his own room.

'William!' Mary called, following him to the door, 'you're not to go on your own. We've still got a Solemn Vow about that.'

'I won't, I promise,' her brother told her.

'He promised before,' Alice remarked, crouching in front of the electric fire once more. 'He broke the Solemn Vow last time. I'm not sure he didn't break it twice.'

'It's all right. I've brought an alarm as well,' Mary told her.

'Well I don't need one,' Alice said, loftily. 'I just tell myself what time I want to wake up and then I do.'

'I bet you can't.'

'Can. How much d'you bet me?'

'If you wake up at quarter to six in the morning, and wake me up to prove it, I'll give you . . . ten p.'

'Ten p?' Alice scoffed. 'It's worth much more than that.'

But, in the end, it was William who had to wake both the girls the following morning. The sun was streaming in through the window and he said that they should hurry because it was much later than he'd intended.

'I thought you were going to set your alarm,' Mary said, pulling on her clothes.

'I did. But, as soon as it started ringing, I switched it off and went back to sleep. It's quarter to seven already. Come on,' and he hurried from the room.

'You said you were going to set yours as well, Mary,' Alice reminded her.

'No I didn't. You were going to wake me, if you remember.'

'For ten p?' Alice exclaimed. 'Not bloody likely!'

'Don't swear, Alice.'

'It's not swearing. It comes into that play . . . '

But Mary had already run out of the room and wasn't listening to her.

The other two were waiting for her inside the hearth when Alice arrived in the hall. As she came down the stairs, William looked up at the gallery to where Jack and Phoebe's closed bedroom door could just be seen.

'I wonder what time they get up,' he whispered.

'Early, I should think,' Mary said. 'Babies need feeding all the time.'

'Oooh! Don't remind me, Mare,' Alice whispered, pulling a face of disgust. Then a thought occurred to her. 'I'm just going to get Spot' she said, running back across the hall and opening the kitchen door.

Spot immediately jumped out to greet her. He'd been standing on the other side of the door listening to their movements and had been desperate to join them, but hadn't wanted to bark in case he woke the others.

'Right. Let's go,' William whispered and, switching on the torch he was carrying, he started to climb up the protruding stone slabs at the side of the hearth. As soon as he reached the ledge, he made quickly for the dark corner and disappeared behind the jutting wall that hid the bottom of the steps. The others followed him, Mary going next and then Alice, with Spot keeping up the rear.

The steps up the chimney were in pitch darkness and William's torch wasn't of use to anyone but himself, because they spiralled so steeply and so narrowly that he was always out of sight. Even Mary, who was following closely behind him, could see no more than a faint glow ahead and Alice could only fumble her way upwards, tripping and feeling her way as best she could. When they'd climbed a short distance Spot pushed past her.

'Let me go ahead,' he growled, quietly. 'I can see in the dark.'

'Lucky thing,' Alice muttered and then, almost at once, she saw the back of Mary's legs climbing the stairs in front of her and she smelt the strong, cold, sooty air of the chimney and heard the clatter of William and Mary's feet on the stone steps and the softer pad of her own paws.

'Oh!' she gasped in a whisper, 'it's happened, Spot. I'm in you.'

'Sssh!' the dog hissed and together they climbed up the steps, seeing the strange opaque shadowy world, filled with vague moving images, that was the only darkness that Spot ever experienced. Rounding yet another turn in the stairs, they came to the wooden door. Mary was holding it open for them and, as they reached her, she looked back:

'Come on, Alice,' she called, and feeling Spot's head in the darkness, she bent down and stroked him.

'I'm here,' Alice whispered and, as she did so, she once again saw only the darkness and felt Spot's body just in front of her.

'Odd,' she thought. 'When I spoke to Mary, I wasn't in you any more, Spot.'

'Don't try and work it out,' Spot whispered in her head. 'Just let it happen.'

'But – how?' she thought, 'when I don't even know what it exactly is that does happen.'

'Just. . . . Don't get in the way,' Spot whispered. 'That's what you humans are always doing; stopping things from happening, by wondering when or how they're going to. Watch . . . ' he hissed and the next instant she was back, looking through the dog's eyes, hearing with his ears, feeling with his paws and smelling with his nose.

'Oh!' she gasped, it took her so by surprise.

'See?', the dog growled quietly.

She didn't really, but she didn't want to spoil the experience, so she remained silent.

'There,' Spot said in her head, 'you're learning. Just say nothing and let the experience take over.'

Alice thought about this for a moment.

'Like reading a book?' she asked.

'How would I know?' the dog growled.

'Well, when you're reading a book and it gets really exciting, you forget about who you are and you sort of are the people you're reading about. Is it like that?'

'I don't know,' Spot replied, irritably. 'I've never read a book. And, besides, you're still trying to work out what happens.'

'Well, of course I am,' Alice retorted. 'It is quite unusual for a girl to be able to see through a dog's eyes and everything, you know. You wait till it happens to you, you'll know what I'm talking about. I can't wait for you to be in me when I go to the dentist or something – then you'll see how odd all this is.'

But Spot merely yawned at the thought and Alice felt her jaw stretch and she lowered her nose and sniffed at the stone step, getting a strong smell of Mary from it.

So they arrived at the top of the spiral and went into the secret room.

'It's dark in here,' William whispered. 'Funny. There should be light coming from the windows.'

He crossed to where one of the candle sconces with the reflector mirror behind it was fixed to the brick of the chimney breast.

'I see,' he muttered to himself, 'the windows have wooden shutters covering them.' And, as he spoke, he unfastened an iron latch and pulled open the two halves of dark wood to reveal the circular window, with the sun blazing outside.

'I don't remember there being shutters before, do you?' he asked, as he swung the round window open on its pivot, allowing the morning breeze to blow into the room.

Alice watched Mary walk towards the window. She seemed immensely tall. She leaned with her hands on the bottom of the circular frame and stood on tiptoes to see out. William stepped back at the same moment, to make way for Mary, and inadvertently stood on Alice, making her leap away with a yelp of pain.

'Sorry, Spot,' he said. 'I wasn't looking where I was treading. Sorry, boy,' and he fondled Alice behind an ear, which had a rather tickly feel and made her put her head on one side.

'Now where's Alice?' Mary said, sounding cross, as she turned back into the room.

'You see?' Spot whispered in Alice's head. 'It's just a matter of letting things happen.'

'But,' Alice thought to Spot, 'what will happen if I reappear? I mean – won't they see me . . . sort of . . . come out of you?'

'I don't know,' the dog growled. 'Try it.'

And, as she finished the thought, Alice saw Spot sitting on the floor immediately in front of her.

'Oh, there you are,' Mary said. 'What kept you?'

Alice frowned.

'Where did I come from?' she asked.

Both William and Mary stared at her, with puzzled expressions.

'Well, you asked where I was, Mary' Alice insisted. 'Then you said . . . oh, there you are. All I'm saying is – where do you think I suddenly appeared from?'

Mary shrugged.

'Up the stairs,' she replied, sounding bored. 'Why are you being so mysterious?'

'You mean you actually saw me come through the door? And cross the room?' Alice challenged her.

'Of course,' Mary said, with another shrug. She was now beginning to sound cross.

'Honestly!' Alice said. 'You didn't see anything of the sort. I was in Spot when I came in. I've just now come . . . out of him.'

The other two blinked at her and looked most confused.

'It's true, isn't it Spot?' Alice insisted.

The dog just remained sitting on the floor, watching her.

'Do it again then,' William told her.

'You've got to believe it, if you're going to see it,' Alice told him.

'But, if I don't believe it – then what would happen?' her brother asked.

'I don't know, do I?' Alice said, sounding peeved. 'I don't know the answers, or how it works or anything. I just know that it . . . somehow happens.'

'Go on, then,' Mary was challenging her now, 'do it again'.

Alice stumped away across the room, feeling cross and frustrated.

'I've told you. I don't know how to,' she said. 'It just . . .'

'Happens?' a voice said and Stephen Tyler walked out of the dark corner opposite to the door and over towards them. 'The difference between magic and science is that magic can't be put to the test. The problem with science is that relying on proof can cloud one's perception of the magic that is ever present.'

Then he walked straight past them all, as if he wasn't aware of their presence, and stood with his back to them, looking out of the window that William had just opened.

'The secret technique depends entirely on stillness,' he mused. 'Yes, that's it! Before you can warm the quicksilver, you must first of all hold it in one piece. It must not be allowed to run or divide. The nature of Mercury is both heavy and active. Only when it is placed in the crucible can you begin to work on it. But beyond such work . . . is the magic. The work is essential, but it will come to nothing, if the magic is not admitted. And where does the magic come from? That is the great question. The question without an answer. Where does the magic come from?' He turned slowly and stared thoughtfully at each of them, as if expecting one of them to give him an answer. 'From the grace of God, perhaps? The scientist finds God an uncomfortable concept because God evades proof. The alchemist, on the other hand, welcomes God into his study, for the alchemist knows that the unanswerable is essential to his art'. He nodded to himself, seeming to think deeply about what he had just said, then shook his head and sighed. 'But the unanswerable questions are, nevertheless, hard to endure. So,' he said, looking at the children again, 'you're here. Good. Good. I did think that we shouldn't meet here. But a man needs his study. I find it difficult to think, let alone materialise, elsewhere. Besides, Morden is away in London. So there is no one to overhear our discourse. Ask your questions now. You, at least are fortunate. The questions you have will be, for the most part, of the answerable variety.'

The children all started talking at once, making so much noise that the old man raised his hands to his ears as if he were being deafened.

'Silence!' he roared, making each of them stop in mid-sentence. 'That's better,' he said in the ensuing silence. 'What a horrible noise. Now – each ask a question in turn.' He turned and glared at William. 'You, boy, you start. You're so full of theories and logic, you must have questions that stretch from here to London. You're only allowed one, mind – so make it a good one.'

William thought for a moment. It was a bit like being given a single wish, you had to be sure it was the best one.

'If, as you say,' he began, 'the alchemy isn't for turning poor metal into gold – then what is it

103

for? I mean – what is our task really for? When we know our . . . true Self, as you call it, what then?'

Stephen Tyler nodded and there was almost a glimmer of a smile on his stern face.

'There you go, William! Just as I predicted. I allow you one question and you ask three.'

'But they're all the same question, really,' William protested.

'No, they are not,' the old man countered. 'They are very different questions that may, I say *may*, in the end lead to the same answer. Now, which is your question?'

William wrestled with all the confusion in his head. It was hard – trying to ask just one simple thing, when there was so much he didn't understand.

'If all we have to do is to get to know ourselves,' he said at last, 'well, what use will that be?'

The Magician answered him quietly.

'A person who really knows him or herself,' he said, 'a person who understands the true potential in Mankind, such a person will leave their mark on the world; for the world will be a better place, just because such a person has lived there. The person who speaks for justice and honour, for compassion and understanding, speaks for all Mankind. The person who acts truly and deals wisely compensates for the base and the evil in Man. Listen to me, William,' and he drew closer to the boy, speaking directly to him, 'one brave act of true compassion can undo a hundred works of the devil; one loving gesture wipes away the tears of humanity. For, at the heart of us all, each and every one of us, there is a grain of pure Gold. That Gold is the Self. That Gold is called Love. It is everyman's birthright.'

'What, even your horrible assistant?' Alice exclaimed.

Stephen Tyler swung round and looked at her.

'Your question is about Morden, is it?'

'Well, no. Not really,' Alice replied, hanging her head.

'But – surely, you have just asked about him?'

'All right, then,' Alice said, sounding braver. 'Why was the rat so horrible at Christmas – and now, why are there men who kill badgers for sport?'

'Badgers?' the old man asked, sounding perplexed. He walked away from them and, when he turned to look at them again, his eyes had a faraway look. 'Badgers!' he repeated as though he'd just had a wonderful idea. 'Good. Good, Alice. Be concerned for the badgers. That's good.'

'But why do men try to kill them? Why does Morden get a rat to make everything horrible?'

'Why, you are asking, is there evil? It is a big question for a small girl.' The Magician thought for a moment. 'There is evil in order that there can be good. Evil is necessary, if good is necessary. One day, perhaps, we will live in a world where evil no longer exists. In which case good will not exist either. Some people refer to this state as a 'Golden Age', perhaps what they really mean is paradise. But, you know, if, in the story, Adam and Eve had not been banished from Eden, would they ever have known how special Eden – paradise – was? You have to lose a thing to want it badly enough. Evil makes good. The one cannot exist without the other. So, never be afraid of evil, Alice. It is a useful property. You and I must talk about this again. It is a very big question. But a good one. It is a question from the heart.'

Alice pursed her lips and looked at her feet.

'I still don't see why men have to go killing badgers,' she muttered.

'No, well . . . ' the Magician said, nodding. 'As I say, it is very difficult. Perhaps you will discover that answer. Oh, and a word of warning,' he continued, peering at them as though he was seeing them from a long distance. 'If you are to continue with this work, it is more than possible that you will be persecuted for it. People do not like their perception of the world to be changed.'

'Is that why the stories about this valley tell of how an evil Magician once lived here?' Mary asked, remembering suddenly Meg Lewis's words to them.

'Is that what they'll say about me after my death?' the old man asked. 'I wouldn't be at all surprised. Perhaps you will be able to . . . correct the stories? I'd be most grateful. One's reputation is so important, don't you think? Or, is that just an old man's vanity? So, Mary, now it is your turn. What is your question for me?'

Mary didn't hesitate. She had decided quite definitely what her question should be.

'Why is Phoebe's baby, Stephanie, so important to you?'

The Magician was silent for a long moment and when he answered her, his voice sounded older and more tired.

'Perhaps here more than anywhere else you will witness an old man's vanity. I was once to have had a child. I was once to have been a father. My wife died in childbirth. I lost them both in one bleak moment.' He shook his head. 'My child was a boy. I would have taught him all I knew. He would have been my future. He would have prospered in the secret arts. He would have achieved what his father will fail to achieve; he would have reached beyond my capabilities.' He was silent, again, lost in his own thought.

'I'm sorry,' Mary whispered. 'I didn't realize . . .'

Stephen Tyler put a hand on her shoulder.

'Don't be sorry. It is good that I tell you. It was all a long time ago. But, imagine my surprise when I discovered that another Tyler had moved into Golden House – the woman Phoebe, living in your time . . .'

'We were right, then,' William exclaimed. 'But Phoebe's surname is Taylor . . .'

'Yes,' the Magician explained, 'names change as time passes. I wanted her to have a boy child . . . for me to influence before I am called away from this life. But, instead, she had a girl, this Stephanie, as you called her. Well, so much for an old man's vanity! Besides, if you two girls are the product of your age – then she will do very well. But it will be for you to train her, not I, for I am already past my time,' he frowned and shook his head, 'and I find that babies are not very receptive to ideas – they're too busy just Being, I suppose!' He stopped speaking for a moment, and then raised a hand, as if a memory had suddenly occurred to him. 'What is the meaning of "O. K."?'

The children were puzzled by his question.

'The meaning of the letters O and K placed together,' he repeated the question, testily.

'Well, OK means sort of . . . OK. You know,' Alice said, with a shrug.

'Little girl, I don't know. That's why I'm asking. Come . . . ' and he beckoned them to follow him. He led them to a dark corner of the room. On the wall was a round mirror, with a convex glass which reflected most of the room.

'This is my glass,' he explained. 'If you ever come to my time, you will discover that where here the glass is convex – and reflects a wide horizon, in my time the glass is concave – like the inside of a bowl – and it reflects back and forth across itself to the inner infinity of absolute nothing.' He nodded. 'It is a little complicated, I see that. But look for yourselves; someone has written on it.'

As the children peered at the dark glass they saw words, written in the dust on its surface.

'What does it say, Will?' Alice asked, reaching up and trying to read it.

'*The Fang Rules – OK*' William read out, in a shocked voice.

'The Fang?' Alice gasped. 'That's the same message that was written on the cellar floor, isn't it?'

'The cellar floor?' Stephen Tyler asked.

Then, before anyone had time to explain, Mary reached across and wiped the mirror clean with the palm of her hand, saying:

'I don't like it. There's something nasty about it.'

'But – who wrote it?' Stephen Tyler asked quietly. 'And why? Who, or what, is "The Fang"?

You will find out for me? The message belongs to your time – it wasn't one of you who wrote it by any chance?'

'No!' Mary exclaimed.

'But you understand its meaning?' Stephen Tyler asked her.

'No, not exactly. But it just seems . . . cruel.'

Stephen Tyler looked at her thoughtfully. Then he nodded and smiled.

'I thought so as well,' he said. 'Forgive me – which one are you?'

'I'm Mary.'

'Yes, that's right. Jasper, the owl, speaks often of you. Good, good. I'm tired now. Being old is a confounded nuisance. If only I'd managed to meet you years ago. Never mind. Old men dwell on "if onlys". That will never do. "The Fang Rules, OK." A fang is a tooth, isn't it? Tt tt tt,' he tutted and turned, looking once more at the mirror.

'What is the date in your time, Mr Tyler?' Mary asked him.

'The date?' he repeated, with his back to them. 'Oh, dear – that sort of detail always taxes me. The date . . . ?'

And suddenly, he wasn't there any more. He went like a light goes when the electric current is switched off; one moment he was present, the next . . . he was not. It took them so by surprise that none of them spoke. They simply stood staring at the vacant space that he'd occupied a moment before. In front of them the mirror, now wiped clean of its message, faced them on the wall. And, as they watched, it seemed as if, for an instant, the other side of the glass was filled by the shadowy form of Stephen Tyler's head.

'Is he looking at us, d'you think?' Alice whispered. But, of course, none of them knew the answer nor did it seem very important. 'He'll come back when he's had a rest, I expect,' she added. 'Actually, I find him quite tiring. I don't understand what he's talking about most of the time. In fact it often seems as though he isn't really speaking to us – more to himself.'

'Who d'you suppose has been up here?' William asked, looking round at the dusty, empty room. 'I mean it has to have been either Jack or Phoebe.'

'They wouldn't write a thing like that, Will,' Mary protested.

'Why was it so horrible?' Alice asked. 'I don't see why it was so horrible.'

'Unless, of course,' William continued, thoughtfully, 'it might have been one of the builders Jack mentioned. They could have found the room when they wre working on the roof.'

'Well, whoever it was, it was a nasty message,' Mary said. 'I can't explain why. It has the same sort of feel as when we saw the dead badger. Sad and senseless and . . . I don't know.' She shook her head. 'It was just vile.'

Spot, who had remained silently watching, crossed to her and licked her hand. This sudden gesture of affection was too much for Mary who felt tears rising in her throat.

'Oh, Spot!' she whispered, bending and kissing him on the head. Then she ran to the door, saying: 'Come on, I'm going down now.'

William crossed quickly to close the shutters.

'Yes, we'd better get down,' he said. 'We don't want to put Phoebe in another temper and it must be nearly breakfast time.'

'Oh,' Alice sighed, 'I'd give anything for some sausages. I bet it's because she only eats vegetables all the time that makes Phoebe so cross.'

11
The Map

'Poor Mr Tyler,' Mary said. 'I wish I hadn't asked him about the baby.'

They were sitting on a bench in the walled garden. A warm sun was shining down. Around them stretched rows of fruit trees, covered with blossom. The air was filled with the singing of birds and the buzzing of bees.

'At least you understood your answer,' Alice said. 'I hadn't a clue what he was saying to me.' Then she sighed, 'Oh, it's like being a prisoner here. I mean, what are we supposed to do all day, if we can't go and explore? Oh, Phoebe! I always hated her, you know. I was the one who thought she was probably a witch . . . '

'Oh, don't go on about it, Alice,' Mary said wearily.

'I wish I'd gone into town with Uncle Jack,' Alice continued. 'At least it'd have been less boring than this.'

'We mustn't waste time,' William announced unexpectedly and, as he spoke, he stood up.

'Where are you going?' Alice asked, jumping up, glad that something was happening at last.

'I won't be a minute,' he called as he hurried towards the house.

'Oh, cup cakes!' Alice swore miserably, and she kicked a pebble along the path, peevishly.

'Al,' Mary said after a moment, 'd'you suppose Mr Tyler is unhappy all the time?'

'I don't know, do I?' Alice asked, sitting down on the bench again and not really listening to her.

'I shouldn't have asked him about the baby . . . ' Mary said again.

But Alice was busy working out a scheme and didn't really hear her.

'Next time Jack goes into town,' she said, 'I'm going with him – and I'm going to spend all my money in a butcher's shop buying really bloody bits of meat . . . and I'm going to parcel them all up and send them to Phoebe. "Oh, lovely!" she'll say, in that stupid voice she uses, "somebody's sent me a present!" and she'll tear open the parcel . . . and all the blood and stuff'll come pouring out all over her and I expect she'll faint or something . . . '

'Alice!' Mary groaned.

'I expect it'll send her right round the bend, and she'll have to be put in a loony bin. Then Uncle Jack can live with another woman instead. Perfect! It's a good job he never married her . . . '

'I wonder where William went,' Mary said, and the two girls fell silent again.

William had gone in search of Phoebe. He found her up a ladder in the first floor bathroom, painting the ceiling.

'Sorry to disturb you, Phoebe,' he said coming in through the door and almost tripping over a tin of paint.

'Careful!' she yelled.

'Sorry,' he said again and then he stood, awkwardly, waiting for her to finish painting a straight line between the wall and ceiling.

'What can I do for you?' she said, concentrating on her work. 'It isn't time for a break yet, surely? You're not hungry, are you?'

'No,' William assured her. Phoebe seemed to think that the only thing any of them ever wanted was food. 'I just wondered . . . You said you were going to get a map for us. Did you remember?'

Phoebe glanced down at him.

'I did, but you won't be needing it now, will you? You're not going anywhere,' she said. 'Where are the girls?'

'Sitting in the walled garden,' William said with a shrug.

Phoebe frowned.

'Don't you want to play or something? Sounds a bit boring to me – just sitting.'

'We don't actually do much playing,' William told her, trying not to let his voice sound disgusted at the thought.

'Oh, William!' she said, pushing some loose hair back from her forehead with the back of her hand and climbing down off the ladder. 'We've got off on the wrong foot again. It isn't meant to be like this. You're supposed to come here and have a lovely holiday and want it to go on for ever . . . I am sorry.'

'It's our fault as well. It was wrong of us to stay out all day.'

Phoebe shook her head.

'I lost my temper, William. I admit it. I should

know better.' Then she smiled at him, as though she was trying to be friendly. 'The least I can do is apologise!' She sighed. 'The map's in the centre drawer of the dresser in the kitchen,' she said.

'Can I take it?' he asked, eagerly. 'It's just . . . I wanted to see where we got lost in the forest yesterday.'

'Yes, of course. I bought it for you.' She picked up the paint tin. 'Jack thinks I'm being unreasonable, anyway, stopping you going out. But then he thinks I'm being unreasonable about a lot of things. Including the builders. That's one of the reasons he's gone into town. To ask them back.' She shrugged and pushed a lock of hair back from her forehead again. 'I know he's right. Of course we need help. Look . . . ' she said, glancing at him, 'maybe . . . after lunch, you could go for a walk . . . if you promise not to go too far.'

'Terrific!' William exclaimed. 'We won't get lost again, honestly. Not with a map.'

'I only stopped you going out for your own good, you know,' she said.

'Yes,' he replied, 'but we're quite grown up really. We don't need . . . watching all the time. Mum and Dad let us explore for miles on our own when we're with them.'

'Yes, sure,' Phoebe said, climbing the ladder once more. 'I'm not used to having children around, that's all.'

'Thanks anyway, Phoebe,' William called, hurrying away.

The girls were still sitting on the bench when he returned, with a look of utter dejection on each of their faces.

'I have never been so bored since that time Mum and Dad took us to Stratford-on-Avon to see Hamlet,' Alice announced as he approached.

'I quite liked Hamlet,' Mary said in a dull voice.

'Everyone knows you're mad, Mary,' Alice told her, pityingly. 'It was the longest, soppiest, most incredibly boring thing I've ever seen in my entire life . . . '

'So, like I was saying,' William interrupted her, 'we've got to treat all this like orienteering.'

'Oh, now what are you talking about, Will?' Alice demanded, close to despair.

'With orienteering,' he persisted, 'you get dropped from a car in a bit of country that you don't recognize and you haven't a clue where you are but, with the aid of a map . . . ' as he spoke, he raised the map he was holding, 'and a compass . . . ' he produced his compass from his pocket, 'and using the landmarks that surround you, you can find your way home.'

'I don't see what that's got to do with anything,' Mary snapped. She really disliked William when he started lecturing.

'Just think about it, Mary. When we were last here, at Christmas, all sorts of incredible things happened but we didn't know why . . . '

Alice sighed, gloomily. She didn't feel like having one of William's long discussions.

'I wonder where Spot is?' she said, looking round. 'I haven't seen him since we were up in the secret room.'

'That's just the sort of thing I mean,' William said quickly.

'What?'

'Things keep happening – or not – and we don't know why. I'm sure that they're like . . . clues and we could learn from them if we could only see how.'

'Spot says,' Alice remembered suddenly, 'that humans are always trying to work things out when really we should just let things happen.'

'But – we are humans,' William protested. 'And we've got human brains that are capable of working things out – so, it's only natural that we should try.'

Alice shrugged and looked sulky.

'I'm just telling you what Spot said.'

'Anyway, I know what he means,' Mary cut in. 'While we're all the time trying to work things out in our heads, we don't notice what's going on round us.'

'With orienteering' William continued 'you have to notice everything – and work out what you're being told at the same time.'

'What's orienteering got to do with anything?' Mary protested.

'Because we have to work out what's going on.'

'If you're so busy thinking,' Mary said, 'you forget to use your other senses. Smell and touch and sight . . . and maybe they can help you to understand as well.'

Alice nodded enthusiastically.

'That's exactly how it was with Spot . . . when I went inside him on the steps up the chimney. When I was just being me, I could only see the dark and I was trying ever so hard to see . . . But, when I went into him, I could see things in the dark and feel the steps and smell the chimney smoke and . . . everything.'

'That's how it was on the Dark and Dreadful path as well,' Mary continued, warming to the subject. 'I expect most people would just have found that path and walked up it and not bothered about anything else. But Spot made me feel . . . the atmosphere of it . . . the . . . ' she shivered and shook her head, 'I don't know what the right word is . . . but it was horrible. You could smell . . . something . . . and feel it. Then when we were down in the crypt – it was the same sensation – as if all of me was feeling the cold . . . only it was more than cold.'

For a moment they were silent. Around them the spring hummed and buzzed and fluttered and moved. All nature seemed to be responding to the warm sun and the soft breeze. Birds flitted from tree to tree and in and out among the young leaves of the fruit bushes, while others perched on the branches, singing blithely. Two butterflies flickered past them, like bright jewels. Somewhere up in the forest a woodpecker was drumming and distantly a dog barked.

'He said we had to get to know the natural world,' Mary said, looking round at the peaceful scene.

'I never knew people killed badgers for sport,' William said, as if he'd only just been told. 'What a horrible thing. I wonder where she lives.'

'Who?'

'That woman we met. Meg Lewis.' As he spoke he opened the map and, crouching down on the ground, he spread it out in front of him.

The girls rose and joined him.

'She said Four Fields,' Mary remembered. 'D'you suppose that's the name of her house?'

The map was large scale. William said it covered only about ten miles in each direction. Golden Valley was clearly marked, cutting a narrow winding cleft through the centre of the country in a more or less north to south direction.

'That's the house,' William said, pointing at a little square with the words *Golden House* written beside it.

'Look!' Alice exclaimed, 'It says *Dovecote* there! How funny. There should be three little dots with William, Mary and Alice written beside them. We're looking at a map of where we are – like if we were suddenly birds, looking down at ourselves.'

'So, yesterday, we went through the gate and up. . . . There!' Mary said, excitedly. 'Look! *Standing Stone* it says . . . and there's the lake we saw.'

'And look,' William pointed at a spot to the left of the lake. 'You see this clear area . . . '

'Four little squares. What are they?' Alice asked.

'They could be fields, I suppose,' William suggested.

'Then that's where she might live.'

'She'd get awfully cold in winter,' Mary said. 'Fancy having to get water from a well.'

'And no electricity,' Alice added. 'She must be awfully poor.'

'I think that dot there,' William said, pointing, 'probably indicates that there's some sort of building that must be her house.'

'What are these funny lines over here?' Alice

asked, pointing to a place on the map at the other side of the lake from the four fields.

William glanced down at the chart of reference. 'It's a quarry,' he said.

'It's got it written,' Mary told them, peering at the small print. '*Blackscar Quarry* and then it says in brackets *Disused*. Oh look, there's a long straight sort of path from the quarry . . . It says *bridleway* . . .'

'What like brides and grooms?' Alice asked.

William shook his head.

'Horses. Somewhere you're allowed to take a horse, I think.' He peered more closely at the map. 'I think we must have crossed it at some point yesterday . . . ' then he looked up at them both. 'You know what it is, don't you?'

Mary nodded.

'The Dark and Dreadful Path,' she said, quietly.

'It just goes to the quarry,' Alice said in a matter of fact voice. 'It was probably once the road to it, d'you think?'

'Maybe,' William agreed.

'And,' Mary said, pointing again at the map. 'There's another bridleway leading from those four fields to the forest track.'

'D'you remember when we were looking for Alice, Mare?' William said. 'We got to that first cliff – where we could look over the forest . . . and we saw two paths cutting through the trees. What was it Spot called them?'

'The Light Path and the Dark Path,' Mary replied.

'I think that must be them,' William said.

'They run on either side of the straight line we saw . . . but that isn't marked, is it?' Mary said.

'Doesn't really need to be,' William said, thoughtfully. 'You don't need a map to find it. You just have to look for the signs.'

'Are those gaps in the trees marked on the map, I wonder,' Alice said, crouching closer. 'Where would they be, Will?'

William moved in beside her and together they searched the sheet of paper.

'I can't see them,' he said.

'But then, maybe they wouldn't be on a map,' Mary said, 'any more than our yew tree would be marked. They'd only be there for those people who knew what they were looking for.'

'What people?' Alice asked.

'Maybe people who were looking for Golden House,' Mary said.

'So you mean the straight line was put there after the house was built?' William asked her.

Mary shook her head and frowned.

'It couldn't have been, could it? The lake was already there – and that stone might be as old as Stonehenge . . . '

'What if . . . ' said Alice, then she hesitated.

'What?' asked William.

'What if the house – or at least the tower bit that belonged to the monastery – was built here so that it would be on the straight line.'

'Yes, that's it!' William whooped excitedly. 'Brilliant, Al! Well done.'

'What?' Alice cried, delighted to be so clever and not at all sure what it was that she'd discovered.

'The line came first,' William said, standing

up. 'For some reason men built the tower here and men built the dovecote here and men placed the standing stone there and men cleared the gaps in the trees there and there . . . because those points all happened to be special . . . and then they noticed that all the special points were on this straight line.'

He sat down on the bench behind them and blinked, stuffing his hands into his pockets.

'So, where does that get us?' he asked.

'Maybe we'd know if we went up in a helicopter,' Alice suggested.

'Or . . .' Mary said quietly, looking up above her head, 'if only we could have a bit of magic . . .'

And out of the limitless blue bowl of the sky above them a kestrel suddenly appeared, wheeling and hovering, watching and waiting.

'Kee! Kee! Kee!' it called, the sound echoing from side to side of the valley.

12
'A Bit of Magic'

'Mr Tyler!' Mary called, running forward and reaching up with her hands.

The Kestrel swooped lower, its wings outstretched and motionless except for the quivering tips that seemed to tread the air like a swimmer in water.

William took a step towards Mary, also watching the sky, and Alice, who was still kneeling on the ground beside the map, raised her head, straining her neck as she gazed up at the bird.

The Kestrel looked down.

The three children looked up.

It was as if they were all mysteriously held together, silent and still. The watching between them was intense. 'Like a string tied us together . . .' was how Mary would later describe it. 'Like adjusting the focus on a microscope,' was William's interpretation, 'until the image is crystal clear . . .'

Then Alice suddenly cried out with surprise.

'Oh!' she gasped.

For a moment, instead of seeing the bird, she had seen the three of them on the ground below her; William and Mary with their faces upturned and she herself, crouching on the ground beside them, staring up.

'Let it happen,' a voice whispered.

'But . . . I don't understand,' William sighed.

'Are we in you?' they heard Mary's voice whisper through their minds.

'Don't ask questions,' the voice trilled, and it was as if each of them had made the sounds. They felt the vibrations in their throats and the high, mournful noise came through each of their mouths.

'Kee! Kee! Kee!'

Flexing their wings they slowly turned into a current of air and were lifted on a gentle thermal. The paths and beds of the walled garden were spread out below them like a drawing pinned to a board. At the centre of the design was the dovecote. From it, the four main paths radiated, like the arms of a cross; one to the yard gate, its opposite number to the forest gate; then the two side arms to the outer perimeter path that followed the four square walls of the garden. This outer path, meeting each of the central paths, cut the garden into four equal squares and these four squares were in turn also divided into four smaller squares by narrow paths. Where each of these paths crossed, a tree had been planted in a small circular bed. The whole layout had a symmetry that was pleasing to the eye and yet, at the same time, was a sensible way of dividing a large space into manageable growing areas for the plants that must once have stocked the garden.

For a moment longer they saw themselves, grouped on the side path near one of the benches, staring up, as if they were part of some painting or photograph. Then, with a single beat of the wings, they soared up into the open sky and the garden grew ever smaller until it looked like a beautifully patterned floor tile or a flag stretched out on the ground.

The breeze was stronger now. It combed through the feathers on their breast and skimmed the top of their sleek grey head. But it wasn't cold, it was more as if the breeze was part of them and not something separate; as if the bird wore the air as a person wears a coat. Then the neck craned forward again, and the eyes, hooded against the light, searched the country below.

They could see the steep rake of the roof of Golden House. The chimneys – with the circular windows of the secret room – were in a direct line with the yard gate into the walled garden. The yard itself, from this high vantage point, seemed more an extension of the original tower of the house and they could see fragments of broken wall and slight ruts and mounds in the earth that suggested that at one time the tower had had other buildings behind it.

'That could explain why Uncle Jack hasn't found the steps down into the crypt,' William thought. 'The way down could have come from somewhere in the yard.'

'But wouldn't that mean that there's more crypt under the yard?' Mary thought.

'Probably,' William responded, without realizing that he hadn't thought of the idea.

'Isn't it odd,' Alice mused. 'It's as though we're all one person. Thinking and everything . . . '

'That's right,' a voice trilled, and the bird sailed higher, spiralling round and round on a thermal of warmer air, 'Kee-ing' with pleasure at the sense of space and freedom.

The steep sides of Golden Valley disappeared into shadows and formed a dark cleft through the trees of the forest. When they were poised high above the yew tree with its secret house, they turned and glided on outstretched wings, sliding down the air until, distantly, the surface of a small lake came into view.

The sun, reflecting on the lake, flashed and sparkled filling the space in front of them with glittering fragments as though a glass bowl had shattered, scattering particles of light. They turned once more on languid wings and rose even higher into the pale blue sky, parting the radiant air so that it dripped and fell away from them like water from a swimmer's arms.

The details on the ground became less well defined. The tips of the trees merged together forming a carpet of variegated green. The lake was immediately below them. Ahead, the chimneys of Golden House reached up out of the dark shadows of the valley. They saw the top of the dovecote, standing between them and the house, and beyond, high up on the crest of the valley side, a cleft in the trees, no more than a scratch on the carpet, was clearly visible. The country beyond gradually dropped away to rolling farmland with hedges, woods, sparkling streams and a distant ridge of steep hills.

Again, as the bird slowly turned, they saw the undulating forest stretching far to the horizon. At one place a clearing in the trees made way for four square fields:

'Like a bit of the garden,' Alice thought.

From the four fields a narrow snake of paler green denoted a path through the forest, passing in a near-straight line to the edge of the escarpment above Golden Valley, before disappearing from sight down into its depths.

Swinging still further round, they saw the country beyond the lake. Here the forest gradually grew sparse and finally petered out into rough moorland which in turn rose upwards to more rugged peaks beyond.

'Mountains,' William whispered.

And still they turned, looking now to the opposite side of the lake. Here once again the forest stretched uninterrupted to a hazy horizon. At one place, dark and mysterious, a jagged cliff revealed the only trace of an ancient quarry and a thin dark path stretched in a straight line from it to the forest track.

Finally, coming full circle, the bird hovered on the air, facing Golden House once more.

'It reminds me of something,' William whispered.

'Stop thinking,' the Kestrel cried.

'But we've got to work things out,' William protested.

'Later,' the bird whistled.

'Later, later,' Mary and Alice thought in unison. And William sighed and remained silent.

The bird's outstretched wings were like the arms of a tightrope artist, reaching out to maintain a balance.

'That's it!' William cried, his words coming out as an excited cry and at once the bird turned its head towards the earth and, folding its wings to the side of its body it dropped like a stone out of the sky.

'Ooooh!' Alice screamed, closing her eyes as the ground hurtled towards her. She could feel the rush of wind stingingly cold against her face and tugging at her body with a force that seemed strong enough to tear her apart. Somewhere along the way she felt as though she'd left her stomach behind her and she gasped as if she'd been struck. Then a wave of nausea overwhelmed her and she reached out with her hands, desperate to find something to cling on to.

The pebbles of the path were rough and warm. She found she was kneeling on all fours, facing the earth, gasping for breath.

'What happened?' she sobbed and, as she spoke, she looked up. Mary was still standing beside her, but now, instead of staring up into the sky, she was doubled up and had both her arms up over her head, as though she was protecting herself from some terrible imminent accident. William, at the same moment, staggered backwards, still staring up into the sky. His legs hit the edge of the garden bench and he fell back into a sitting position, his mouth open as if he was trying to scream but was unable to make any sound.

'What happened?' Alice said again.

In front of them, out of the air, the Kestrel dropped to the earth, claws outstretched, silent and deadly. From the centre of a patch of tall grasses it lifted the tiny, wriggling body of a mouse. Holding the squealing creature securely, the bird flew away over the garden wall and disappeared from view.

'Wow!' William exclaimed. Then he shook his

head, no words seeming adequate to express what he wanted to say.

'Has it gone?' Mary asked, her eyes closed again.

'Yes,' William said. 'Didn't you see? It caught a mouse.'

'What happened?' Alice said for the third time, her voice rising into surprised disbelief. 'I mean – we were up there. We were, weren't we? You both felt it, didn't you?'

'But I saw us standing here,' William protested.

'Who saw us?' Alice demanded. 'I did and you did and Mary did. But how? How could we all be up there and down here at the same time? Oh, will somebody please tell me what happened?'

Beyond the wall, in the yard, Spot suddenly started to bark and a moment later the sound of a motor announced the return of Uncle Jack.

'It must be nearly lunch time,' William said, glad to be able to change the subject, and he rose and hurried towards the gate.

'Mary,' Alice said in a small voice. 'Why won't Will talk about it?'

'I think maybe he's afraid.'

'Of what?'

'Of not being able to explain what's happening,' her sister replied.

'But that's so stupid. None of us can.'

'I know,' Mary said, turning to follow William out of the garden. 'But it's worse for him. You know what he's like. He has to be able to work things out. When he can't . . . he gets all moody.'

'All the same,' Alice said, following her, 'I'd

like to know what is going on. I mean – how did it happen, Mare?'

'I don't know how,' Mary said with a shrug. 'But . . .'

'What?' Alice asked.

'Well . . . Maybe it was just a bit of magic,' she replied, quietly. 'Like I wished for.'

'Oh, of course it was,' Alice wailed. 'I know that!'

'Well, you can't explain magic, can you? It just . . . happens,' Mary said and she put an arm round Alice and walked with her through the gate.

13
Alice Goes It Alone

Alice pulled on her jeans and searched in the dark for her sweater. She didn't know what time it was but she could hear Mary breathing steadily and deeply in the next bed and, outside the window, the sky was dark.

She picked up her trainers and tiptoed across to the door. As she opened it, Mary stirred in her sleep.

'What's that?' she muttered.

'It's all right,' Alice whispered. 'It's only me.' Then she slipped out of the room on to the landing and closed the door behind her.

William's door was ajar. She could hear him snoring quietly inside. She went into the bathroom and switched on the light. By leaving the bathroom door open she was able to see dimly into the interior of William's room. His torch was on the bedside table. She crept stealthily across the room, picked it up and carried it back with her out on to the landing. Then, after closing William's door and switching off the bathroom light, she ran lightly down the spiral steps to the gallery and on down the broad stairs to the hall below.

Spot was asleep in his basket, but he sat up as

soon as she entered the kitchen and padded over to greet her, with his head on one side and his tail wagging slowly, as though he was asking what she was up to.

Alice put a finger to her lips and beckoned him to follow her. They went quickly across the hall and into the chimney. As they started to climb up the protruding slabs to the ledge, the clock in the kitchen chimed four.

Alice led the way up the chimney with the thin beam from the torch picking out the steps in front of her. When she reached the wooden door she pulled it open and held it for Spot. She felt his warmth as he squeezed past her and let her hand run lightly along the length of his back, glad of his company and wanting to tell him so. The dog looked back over his shoulder and gave her fingers a reassuring lick. Then, together, they continued the steep climb to the top of the chimney.

The secret room was in darkness. Alice crossed to the front window and reached up to unfasten the wooden shutters. But the clasp was out of her reach. She looked round, hopefully, for something to stand on. But the room was empty of all furniture except the round mirror fixed to the wall in the corner.

'You know,' she whispered to Spot, 'the first time we came up here, last Christmas, I'm sure the room was full of furniture . . . all cluttered and cobwebby. I'm sure it was.'

'That was then,' the dog growled.

'But – where has the furniture gone?' she whispered.

'This is now,' the dog growled.

Alice sighed and shone the torch at his head

for a moment. Then she frowned to herself. Spot could sometimes be really maddening. He had a way of seeming to know things that she didn't, but of not telling her what they were. She could see his eyes glowing in the beam as he stared deeply at her. Then he blinked and turned away from the light as though it was dazzling him.

'Sorry,' she whispered, and she stroked his head, lovingly, and sat down on the floor beside him and shivered. It was cold in the room. For a moment she wished she was back in bed and that she hadn't decided to go it alone.

'But I had to,' she explained to Spot. 'William's gone all moody. I don't think he can cope with the magic, somehow; and Mary . . . well, she's all right, but she seems to think that we have to wait for things to happen to us. I'm sure that's not right. I'm sure we're meant to make our own adventures as well.' Then she smiled and changed the subject, saying excitedly; 'When we were flying, it was really fantastic, Spot. Have you ever?'

'Flown?' the dog said, looking round at her, with a shocked expression. 'Certainly not. I'm a dog.'

Alice got up and walked across to the mirror in the corner and stared thoughtfully up at it.

'It was like nothing I've ever had happen before,' she continued, speaking more to herself than to Spot. 'It was like every ride you've ever been on at the funfair and yet quite different at the same time. Because it was . . . quiet. You know how at the fair everything is noisy? Well, you probably don't know, but it is, anyway. Well, when we were flying it was the opposite. It was quiet, except for the sound of the breeze and . . . ' she frowned again, trying to remember precisely what it had been like. 'I think we could hear birds sometimes and the Kestrel talking – oh, and when one of us thought . . . we could all hear it . . . '

'Ssssh!' the dog hissed, sharply.

'What?' Alice asked, stopping in mid stream and listening intently.

'That's better,' Spot growled.

'What, Spot?' she asked him, puzzled. 'What is it? I can't hear anything.'

'Precisely,' the dog said. 'I've never known so much talking. No wonder the Magician finds it hard to get through.'

'Through?' Alice asked.

'While you're chattering all the time, you miss the important things,' Spot explained, then he stretched himself and settled down again with a sigh of contentment.

Alice pulled a face and turned her back on him. Even Spot was being more irritable than usual with her. He was supposed to be her friend, but he nagged her just like William. She sighed and put her hands behind her back, switching off the torch as she did so. But, as the beam went out, the light didn't entirely disappear. For a moment Alice thought that the sun must have risen and that the daylight was finding a way through the shutters, but looking back over her shoulders she saw that the room behind her was in total darkness. What little light she had noticed was coming from the corner of the room.

Turning slowly, and feeling her heart beginning to race, she looked towards the mirror. The glass glowed dully in the dark. She took a step towards it, surprised at what she saw. The circular wooden frame contained an area of light that was growing stronger as she watched. She moved closer, until she was standing directly in front of the mirror. It hung on the wall at a height above the level of her head, but not so high up that she wasn't able to look into it with ease. At first all she saw was the strange glow that gradually suffused the room in which she stood. It was a bit like standing outside a house with curtains drawn across the windows, so that although you knew that there was light within, you were unable actually to see into the rooms.

Alice stared at the glass, transfixed, as the light grew stronger – like the sun rising imperceptibly over the edge of the horizon – until, at last, it was strong enough for her to be able to see the room on the other side. It was a steeply pitched attic with a door at one end, leading out into a dark space. To the right and left of the door, high up in the roof, were two circular windows. Candles were burning in sconces in front of both the windows and behind the candles were circles of burnished metal, so that the light from them was intensified. There was a lantern burning on a low table, and a log fire glowing and sometimes erupting into flame in a small hearth.

Alice recognized at once that it was the room that she was standing in. But it wasn't a reflection she was looking at because she couldn't see herself in the glass and besides the room was altogether different. Through the mirror, the room was furnished and lived in, whereas on the side she was standing it was forever empty and abandoned.

Then, just as she was beginning to admire all the different features – the shelves of books, the strange, globe-like ornament on a side table, the bottles and jars, the piles of manuscripts on the desk and charts pinned to the wall – Stephen Tyler appeared through the door she could see at the back of the room. He was breathing heavily and he leaned on his silver stick as though he was exhausted by the steep climb up the steps in the chimney.

14
The Swallows Have Come

'Ah! There you are,' the Magician said, coming into the room.

Alice turned quickly and discovered him walking from the door to the front window.

'But . . . ' she gasped.

'But?' he queried, opening the shutters. 'But? What sort of a welcome is "but"?'

Spot rose from the floor and sauntered over to him, with his tail wagging.

'You were . . . I saw you in the mirror . . . '

'My reflection. You saw my reflection,' he told her, stroking the dog's head with the back of his hand.

'No,' Alice insisted. 'It wasn't like that. I saw you through the mirror, coming into that room. You were there and . . . '

'And now I am here.'

'No. You don't understand. Here and there were quite different. I was looking in the mirror and I saw this room . . . but with furniture and . . . and the fire was alight and . . . candles . . . I saw you come into the room . . . but not this empty room . . . '

Stephen Tyler walked slowly over to her and put a hand on her shoulder.

'I know. I know,' he said gently. 'It is very, very confusing. I find it to be so myself. It is all to do with time. Layers of . . . time. I'm sure I've explained this before.'

'Oh, you've explained it,' Alice said, rather crossly. 'Or rather, you've talked about it. But,' she shrugged and pulled a face, 'I'm not sure I ever understand anything you say. Not really. I expect William does. But I don't,' and she shrugged again and walked away from him, wishing that Spot would come and join her instead of sitting at the Magician's feet in such an adoring fashion.

'I'd better try again, then,' the Magician said, using a patient voice, that made Alice feel more cross than ever. 'This room is both furnished and not furnished, ruined and not yet built . . . The perception of it depends entirely upon where you are looking from.'

'Perception?' Alice asked, wearily. 'Long words may be clever, but they don't help, you know.'

'Sorry,' the Magician said, now sounding contrite. 'Perception means . . . Well, I wonder what it does mean. The seeing of an object or event; or the recognition of it; the becoming aware of it in one way or another. It is the same with most things, you know. The perceiving of magic is very similar. If you find you are flying as a kestrel . . . you must just fly! If your mind says "this cannot be, it isn't possible" . . . then that thought may just persuade you that what is taking place isn't possible. Then what would happen?'

'We'd come whizzing out of the sky and end up where we started from – in the walled garden.'

'Yes,' Stephen Tyler nodded, 'that could be how it seemed to you. In fact all that happened was that the magic stopped.'

'So – what are we supposed to do?'

'Nothing! Do . . . nothing. Just allow things to be. Don't interfere. Don't . . . get in the way. It's really perfectly simple. Do you know how you breathe? Do you know how your body functions? Do you know where dreams and ideas and inspirations and laughter and tears and feelings come from? Of course you don't. Start asking how? and where? and why? . . . and you could stop the lot. Then where would you be?'

Alice pulled a solemn face.

'Dead, I suppose, if I stopped breathing,' she said.

'Yes,' the Magician said with an emphatic nod, then he frowned and seemed to consider the statement, ' . . . and at the same time, maybe no. The concept "death" is very complex.'

'Concept?' Alice snapped the word, as an irritated question.

'Idea,' he replied.

'Well, then . . . ' Alice began, but he held up his hand and silenced her.

'You are absolutely right to protest. Words are inadequate and long words are more inadequate than most. I have not very often had the privilege of conversing with a mind as untrammelled as yours . . . '

'What?' Alice shook with frustration. 'There you go again! Ooooh!' and she stamped her foot and walked away from him. 'It's worse than useless when you talk to me like that. Because I don't understand what you're saying.'

The Magician immediately looked dejected and Alice felt almost sorry for him.

'Can't you see what it's like for us?' she said. 'We're not used to all this. We go to school and eat sausages and have a perfectly normal life most of the time. Then, all of a sudden we're here. Things "happen" as you say . . . But we don't know what's going on, or why. We don't know what we're supposed to do, or think or anything. It really is a bit weird, you know. And you're the only one who can explain things to us and when you start to . . . you use words that don't mean anything – not to me, anyway. Oh, please, Mr Tyler' she said, surprising herself with the intensity of her feelings. 'I really do want to understand and I am trying, honestly I am. But . . . this time it isn't going how I thought it would at all. William is in such a muddle that he's gone into one of his working-out moods; Mary is . . . oh, I don't know what Mary's doing. She'll probably cut her hair quite soon and ask to borrow Phoebe's make-up – if she wears any, which I don't suppose she does . . . What would a vegetable want to look pretty for? Anyway, when Mary goes quiet she usually decides to change her image. You should have seen her when she went Gothic. She wore black eye shadow and black nail varnish at school. She was called in by Miss Atterton and made to wash it all off and . . . '

'Little girl!' the Magician cried, putting his

hands to his ears. 'Stop! You are now making about as much sense to me and as much noise as a duck would do if it tried to sing plainchant.'

'What?' Alice cried. 'A duck? What's a duck got to do with anything?'

'About as much as black shadows and Gothic images and vegetables looking pretty have,' Stephen Tyler snapped. Then he sighed. 'This is without hope,' he said. 'Utterly without hope.'

'When you met us last Christmas, you told us we had important work to do. And then, yesterday, you said so again. Well, why can't we get on and do it?'

'But you are. Don't you see? This is it,' Stephen Tyler cried. 'I have come from another age and I am speaking to you. You are my eyes and my ears. I am experiencing through you. It is all . . . most remarkable.'

'But I want adventures and . . . magic,' Alice exclaimed. 'Not hanging around the house with Phoebe in a bad mood and Uncle Jack too busy to really bother with us. And another thing,' she continued her words coming out faster as she grew in confidence. 'William says that we're bound to want to work things out – because we're humans . . . and that's what humans do best.'

The Magician nodded.

'Well then?' Alice demanded.

'It is, as I told you, very confusing. The problem is the magic. Over that we have little control . . . '

'Not even you?' Alice demanded.

'Oh, to an extent, perhaps. I know how to make certain things come about . . . but I have no control over the events themselves. I cannot make the spring turn to autumn, nor the day to night. In magic, as in life, nature and her laws will always have to be obeyed. And that is what you are learning . . .'

'I am?' Alice asked, surprised at the suggestion. She didn't feel that she was learning anything at all and nor was she sure that she wanted to. Learning sounded far too close to school work, and it was the holidays after all.

'You particularly,' Stephen Tyler told her. 'The others – your brother and sister – will take longer. The boy, William, is all head. But I will crack him open, given time. And the other girl . . . Mary, is it? She is all heart, and that is going to take longer. Longer, but she will be most effective when her time comes. But you, little girl . . .'

'I wish you wouldn't call me that,' Alice interjected. 'I really hate it. I'm only little because I'm the youngest and as far as being a girl is concerned . . .'

'Be quiet!' Stephen Tyler thundered and his eyes flashed with anger and he raised his silver stick as though he would strike her with it.

'Well,' Alice continued, but in a less confident and much lower voice. 'How would you like it if I called you "old man" all the time?'

'I should hate it,' Stephen Tyler replied and he looked at her and smiled. 'I like you, Alice.'

'That's the first time you've used my name, I think.'

'It is a good name.' He looked sad for a moment, then he shook his head. 'You are like a slate waiting to be written on. Youth is a wonderful state to be in. The tragedy is that we never know it at the time.'

He crossed and looked out of the circular window at the front of the house. A breeze was blowing that stirred his hair. In the silence that followed, the first distant singing of birds could be heard and the glimmer of dawn light seeped into the room.

'You're sad now,' Alice said, crossing towards him.

Spot turned and looked at her, his tail moving slowly from side to side on the floor behind him.

'Alchemy makes one sad.'

'I don't even know what that is,' Alice sighed. 'The Alchything, I mean. William said it was turning things into gold. But you got cross with him . . .'

'I did?' Stephen Tyler asked, looking puzzled.

'At Christmas, when we first met you. But if it isn't for turning things into gold . . . What is it? What is what you do . . . for?'

'I tried to explain yesterday. It's more like turning people into gold,' the old man said in a quiet voice.

'People?' Alice gasped. 'I don't want to be turned into gold!'

'No?'

'No. I'd be a statue. I don't want to be a statue.'

The Magician shook his head slowly, looking at her.

'The gold I speak of is a symbolic word . . .' He raised his hand, interrupting Alice's protest. 'A

143

symbol is a word used to represent something else. Like a colour is used in a picture . . . to suggest depth and distance on what we really know to be a flat canvas. The study and practice of alchemy focuses the mind and gradually transforms it from its gross state of ordinary, habitual thinking, dependent as it is on action and reaction, preparing it instead for higher understanding, for inspiration and, ultimately, for universal knowledge. As gold is to mud, so is this new mind to our ordinary, everyday one.'

Alice sighed. She had tried so hard to listen to him, but all that he had done was say a lot of meaningless words again.

'You should tell William,' she said, glumly. 'I expect he'd understand.'

'No, Alice,' Stephen Tyler said, gently. 'You'll be first. You don't have to understand. Far better to live it. You'll be first because you can imagine . . . Imagination is all important.' He beckoned to her. 'Come and see,' he whispered, turning and looking out of the window.

'I can't,' Alice said. 'It's too high for me.'

'Come to me,' he said, beckoning to her again. 'I will hold you.'

Alice put her hands on the bottom rim of the circular window and the Magician lifted her up until she was peeping over the sill. The steep slope of the roof dropped away in front of her and, beyond, the dark trees of the forest crowded up the hillside.

Out in the space between, a bird suddenly darted across her view. Then another plummeted out of the sky, wings spread and the long pointed outer feathers of its tail forming a perfect V-shape.

'The swallows have come,' Stephen Tyler said. 'Bringing summer with them from distant shores beyond our valley.'

As he spoke, more and more swallows came into Alice's view. They skimmed and swooped and dived and soared, filling the air with movement. As though in a secret dance or a special game they managed never to hit one another, although they seemed always on the point of doing so. A bird would turn away from the main throng and whip out into space only to wheel in mid-flight and dive back into the centre of the flock. Then, at the final moment, just as collision seemed inevitable, it would break and either soar upwards into the high sky or downwards towards the grassy earth, before turning once more to hurl itself into the centre of the throng.

It was such a joyful, happy sight that Alice found herself longing to be able to join in.

'You can, if you want to,' Stephen Tyler whispered in her ear.

'But how?' she pleaded with him.

'Just . . . be silent. Let your thoughts rest on the birds. See with their eyes. Look how the sky rushes towards you and the earth withdraws. Feel with their touch. How strong the breeze is; how cold the upward flight, how much warmer when you turn for the earth. Listen . . . can you hear the voices of all your companions? Don't fight it, Alice . . . don't resist. Just . . . imagine . . .'

15
The Builders Return

Alice came in through the yard door just as Mary and William entered the kitchen from the hall.

'There you are,' Mary said. 'Where've you been?'

'Out,' she replied with a shrug.

Her hair was ruffled and her cheeks shining, as though she'd been running. Mary looked at her closely and suspiciously. You could usually tell when Alice had been up to something by the way she avoided your eyes.

'Out where?' she demanded.

'Just out,' Alice replied and she went quickly towards the hall door. 'I'm going up to clean my teeth. I won't be a minute.'

Towards the end of breakfast an old white van drove into the yard and Jack got up from the table, explaining as he went out, that it would be the builders arriving.

The sound of a dog barking made Spot sit up, his head on one side, all the hairs on the back of his neck bristling.

'Oh! They've brought that dog,' Phoebe said, speaking to herself and sounding immediately irritated.

Spot growled quietly, standing facing the back door, with his tail between his legs.

'What's the matter?' Mary asked him.

'He hates the builder's dog as much as I do. It's a real brute,' Phoebe explained.

Jack remained in the yard talking to the builders and when the children went out to join him he introduced them. There were three of them; an older man, called Arthur, who was almost bald and very skinny. He had a sharp pointed nose and pale, shortsighted eyes with the most miserable expression, as though he was always disappointed about something. Then there was Kev. Kev was the complete opposite to Arthur. He was a big, burly man, with short cropped black hair and tattoos on his arm. He wore a vest and his stomach bulged above the belt of his jeans. His face was round and shiny, with red cheeks and an even redder, small, button of a nose. The third builder was a young lad, no more than seventeen, called Dan. Dan was thin with very long legs, emphasized by the tight, torn, jeans that he wore belted with a piece of string. His hair was long and sandy coloured and he wore it tied back in a pony tail.

In the back of the white van a huge, ugly looking dog was tied by a length of rope. It growled at the children and started to bark when Spot appeared behind them at the kitchen door.

'Shut your noise, animal!' Kev shouted. The dog stopped barking at once, but continued to growl menacingly, as it paced the back of the van staring down at Spot and the children.

'So you've come to help us, have you?' the old man, Arthur, said to the children.

'No such luck!' Jack exclaimed. 'They seem to think they're on holiday here.'

'So, what's to do now, then?' Dan asked, turning his back on the children.

'We can start plastering in the Tudor wing,' Jack told them, sounding businesslike. 'Oh! And I've hired a skip, so that we can clear the rubbish from the cellars. It should be delivered later this morning, and it's being collected tomorrow evening.'

'You'll never get all that rubbish into one skip,' Kev told him. 'Nor will we clear it all in a couple of days.'

'Well, at least we can make a start,' Jack countered, patiently.

'I don't mind helping,' William said.

'Wonderful! The more the merrier. I'll accept any unpaid labour that's offered,' Jack rejoined.

'Oh, William!' Mary said. 'I'm not going to spend the day clearing rubbish.'

'You don't have to. I wasn't speaking for you,' William snapped.

'I'll help you, Uncle Jack,' Alice said, quietly.

'No. I wasn't being serious. You lot go off and enjoy yourselves,' Jack told them.

'I'd like to,' Alice protested. This wasn't really true. The last thing Alice wanted to do was to spend the morning dragging piles of rubbish out of the cellar, but she needed time to think. She knew if she spent the day alone with William and Mary she'd end up telling them about her meeting with Stephen Tyler and she wasn't ready for that yet. William would apply logic and explain it away and Mary would feign indifference, which would be almost worse. So, instead, she decided to keep the events of the morning to herself until they were at least clear in her own mind.

'Well,' Jack said, still sounding doubtful, 'if you're really sure you want to.'

'I am,' Alice replied, 'it'll be fun!' And, as she spoke, she watched the swallows skimming above the yard in the free blue sky and she felt the wind on her cheeks and she had to look away quickly for fear of taking off.

'Alice?' Uncle Jack said, putting a hand on her shoulder.

'What?' she asked, breathlessly.

'Are you feeling all right? You look . . . as though you might be running a temperature.'

'No. I'm fine, really,' she replied brightly. 'Where shall we start?'

'By putting on your oldest clothes,' Jack told them. 'We are about to get exceedingly dirty!'

And so, much to Mary's continued disgust, it was agreed that they would spend the morning clearing the cellars and that they'd go out in the afternoon, if they felt like it.

It was hot and tiring work. Mary and Alice were given the job of sorting through the mounds of rubbish in each of the cellars and putting them into piles. William joined Jack and Kev carrying the stuff, load by load, up the cellar steps and along the passage to the main hall and out of the front door to the porch where they made new piles, in readiness for the arrival of the skip.

Arthur and Dan, meanwhile, started plastering ceilings in the rooms off the passage. Dan had a ghetto blaster with him and the house, that had been so silent before their arrival, thrummed to the sound of pop music.

The rubbish in the first room mainly consisted of empty bottles which Mary and Alice put into black plastic bags, but which were then left in the cellar because Jack said there was a bottle bank in the town and he'd take them with him in the Land-Rover the next time he went in.

The second room was where the old suitcase was. It was one of several, all crammed with decaying clothes. There were boxes of hats and a trunk filled with bits of fabric from long ago, that turned into dust as the girls inspected it. Here there were piles of papers tied up with string, there was an assortment of rusty garden implements, old pans, a tea chest filled with a whole dinner service, most of it in good repair, boxes of rusty knives and forks, an ancient iron boiler, several broken chairs, rotting velvet curtains, a tin box crammed to the lid with buttons that fell and scattered across the floor as Alice forced it open.

They went through everything, keeping back anything that might be useful.

In what seemed like no time at all, Phoebe called them up for lunch and the builders went and sat in the van and ate sandwiches while Jack and the children had a salad in the kitchen with Phoebe. The window was open and the sound of Dan's music filled the room. Phoebe wanted Jack to tell him to switch it off, but Jack said it wasn't doing them any harm and why shouldn't he listen to music – if that's what you could call it. Mary informed him that the particular tape he was playing was one of the top bands of the moment and her foot tapped out the rhythm all the time she was eating. At one point, in a lull in the music, they all heard Arthur say:

'Anyone want this corned beef butty?'

'Yes – please,' Alice sighed, with feeling, which made Mary giggle.

'Go on, then, I'll have it,' they heard Kev say, and, as he spoke, he belched loudly. 'Pardon my French!'

This was too much for Alice, who got a fit of the giggles that went slowly right round the table until even Phoebe was shaking with silent laughter and Jack had to get up and close the window for fear of them being overheard.

Once lunch was over, Jack announced that the children were now on official holiday and that they were released from duty. But they all wanted to carry on with the clearing.

'I'm quite enjoying it,' Mary said, to her own amazement.

'Are you getting through it?' Phoebe asked.

'We're keeping back more than we're throwing out,' Mary told her.

'Oh dear,' Phoebe sighed. 'That wasn't the idea at all!'

During the afternoon they started to clear the third cellar. Here was a much less exciting hoard, though Jack seemed delighted with what they found; piles of oak floorboards and old doors.

'From the rooms on the other side of the hall, I expect' he said, 'when they converted them to the Georgian style.'

'Will we keep them?' William asked and he was relieved when Jack said they certainly would.

William was beginning to find the long trek to the front door exhausting.

'It's all right for you two,' he told the girls. 'You're having all the fun.'

'You stay down for a bit, Will,' Jack told him as he and Kev between them carried the shell of a cupboard – without any doors and riddled with woodworm – out of the room.

So William stayed with the girls and between them they found, in a dark corner, leaning against the wall, some metal objects which didn't at once suggest their original usage. There was an iron post with holes at one end that might have been used to fix it in some way to another surface. The other end of this post was pointed. It was almost like a short thick spear. Beside it, on the ground, was another object in the form of a cross, with a hole at its centre. The end of each arm of the cross had a circular disc attached.

'What's it for?' William asked, thoughtfully.

Then Mary found, leaning further along the wall and half obscured by a panel of oak, a third and much larger piece.

'Oh, look!' she said in an excited whisper.

It was also made of wrought iron. A large, flat sculpture, almost. There was a straight rod at its centre. To one side of this rod, and attached by two thin metal arms, was a round sun with pointed rays that stuck out from it like the spokes of a wheel. To the other side of the rood, similarly attached, was a thin shape of a new moon.

'What have you got there?' Jack said, coming into the room suddenly.

'I don't know,' William answered. His voice sounded almost afraid.

'Let me see,' Jack said, moving closer. 'Hey! That's the same design as that pendant I gave Phoebe for Christmas. You remember – the one I found in the hall fireplace. Isn't that weird? Now what in the world is this for?' he frowned, staring thoughtfully at the strange object.

'I think I know,' Mary said quietly.

'What Mare?' Alice asked.

'I think it's like those weather cocks you have on church steeples.'

'Brilliant!' Jack exclaimed. 'That's exactly what it is. It's a weather vane! The design is obviously special to this house. I wonder where it was fixed and why it was taken down. Probably fell off in a gale!'

When Jack and Kev left them again, carrying a rusty tin trunk between them, William turned and looked at the girls.

'You know what else it's like, don't you?' he said. 'One of those drawings from the book Jack borrowed last Christmas. It's to do with alchemy. It's the same design that I thought I saw on the chimney breast, the night I found the steps up the chimney. It's the Magician's emblem, isn't it? We ought to put it back, wherever it belongs. But how will we know where?'

'We could ask him,' Alice said.

'Yes,' William said, quietly, and then he frowned.

'Don't try and work it out, William,' Alice begged him. 'Please.'

'It's just that it seems important and I don't

know why or what it means or . . . anything,' William said. 'I have to know what it represents. I'm not even sure that it is a weathercock. If it was there'd be N, S, E and W on these metal arms instead of which there are only these funny discs,' and he flicked one of the discs with his finger and was surprised when it spun on its axis. 'Hey!' he exclaimed, 'that's even odder, these things move – look!' and he rotated the disc again.

'Well, if it isn't a weathercock – then what is it?' Mary said.

'I don't know, do I? That's the problem,' and not wanting to have another argument, he turned to walk out of the cellar only to find the door blocked by Spot, who was standing listening to them, with his head on one side and his ears forward.

'I'm going to start clearing up in the next room.' William said, pushing past the dog.

'Not without us, William,' Mary said, hurrying after him. 'This is our job, you know,' and she disappeared down the passage.

Alice crossed to the door and flung her arms round the dog's neck.

'Oh, Spot!' she sighed. 'Why does William have to make everything so complicated?'

'Because,' the dog whispered in her ear, in a voice that sounded awfully like Stephen Tyler's, 'that is his nature.'

'But it's wrong, isn't it?' Alice thought.

'No,' the dog voice whispered in her head, 'not for him.'

'But, I thought we weren't meant to try and work things out,' she protested.

'You're not. But you're all different, you know. You are as different from each other as a fish is different from a bird and a bird is different from a bear. Could a bird swim? Could a bear fly? Don't try to make other people like yourself, Alice. Try rather to discover who you really are.'

'Then what?' she thought, glumly.

'Then you will be like yourself – and no one else,' the answer came to her. 'You will be . . . yourself. When that time comes . . . then the alchemy will have taken place. Then you will indeed be . . . gold.'

16
The Lights In The Dark

Alice swooped through the warm air. She had never felt so happy in the whole of her life. The sensation was rather like swimming or being on an endless big dipper at a fun fair. The early sun beat down from a clear sky and below all the trees of the forest glittered with dew as if they'd been dusted with diamonds. Her companions, the other swallows, were so full of joy that they filled the space around her with twittering laughter. Alice wanted nothing more than to fly and skim and whiz through the morning light for ever. She turned and, with a tremendous spurt of energy, thrust herself upwards, parting the air with her sharp wings as if she was trying to reach the sun itself. The light was so dazzling that she felt herself merging into the sky. In the final moment, just when it seemed that she would disappear for ever into the vast blue distance, she turned again and careered towards the earth, like an arrow shot from a bow.

The ground sped towards her. Trees parted, bushes brushed her, the tall grass enveloped her like a jungle.

'Alice! Alice!' she heard a voice calling to her from far away.

'What?' she said and, at the same moment, she opened her eyes. The room was in darkness. Then she heard the voice again:

'Alice, wake up,' it said.

At first she couldn't remember where she was. She wanted to go back to sleep and fly with the swallows. But Mary was kneeling on the ground beside her bed, gently shaking her and sleep slipped away.

'What's happened?' Alice asked, alert and a little frightened.

'There's something funny going on. Come and look,' Mary whispered.

Alice climbed out of bed and followed her sister out of the room and across the tiny landing to the bathroom.

'It was the barking that woke me up,' Mary explained and, as she did so, Alice heard a sharp, staccato sound coming from beyond the bathroom window. 'But then I came out here and – look!' Mary continued.

At first the view from the window was only a blank wall of night but, as Alice watched, she saw for a moment a light flickering in the darkness. It came and went so fast that at first she was hardly sure that she'd really seen it. But then it reappeared again at a slightly higher level.

'What is it?' she whispered.

'Someone up on the side of the valley. Near where we were when we found the tree house, I think. Look – there's another light, over to the right.'

As the girls watched, the two lights gradually came together and a ferocious growling mingled with the barking.

William came into the room behind them.

'You've seen it?' he whispered. 'I was coming to wake you.'

'William, you're dressed!' Alice whispered.

'Yes. You'd better hurry,' he told them. 'Put on sweaters. It'll be cold out there.'

'We're going out?' Alice asked, surprised.

'Well, I am. I want to know what's going on. If you're coming, you'd better hurry,' and, as he spoke, he flicked on the torch he was carrying, lighting their way back to the bedroom.

The night air was cold as they let themselves out of the kitchen door and hurried across the yard into the walled garden. Spot bounded ahead of them, as if he knew immediately what was going on. Then he waited for them by the back gate and, as they went out on to the forest track, he turned, jumping up and down, with his tail wagging.

'All right, we'll follow you, Spot,' Mary whispered. 'But we must go carefully – whoever it is may not be friendly. We just want to see what's going on, that's all.'

Spot led the way along the track and then turned, following a narrow path that climbed through the trees up the steep side of the valley.

Although they were travelling at quite a speed, Alice was able to keep up with the others. William used the torch as little as possible, only flashing it on for brief moments if the ground became particularly uneven or an obstacle presented itself. Once they were in amongst the trees, they were unable to see the moving lights any more, but the occasional sharp bark told them that they were drawing closer to their goal.

Eventually, after about fifteen minutes of stiff climbing, the trees around them began to thin. They could see the crest of the hill with the great, dark shape of the yew tree billowing up out of the surrounding shadows and silhouetted against the sky.

The rising ground was very precipitous here and the path disappeared altogether. Spot, ahead of them, slowed his pace to an apprehensive prowl, his paws rising in slow motion, his head straining forward, as he probed the half-darkness with all his senses.

Then, suddenly and unexpectedly, a voice broke the stillness.

'Who's there?' it whispered, urgently. 'Ted?'

The children froze. The ground in front of them was so steep that they were clinging to the side of the hill.

'Over here!' a more distant voice called.

Above them and a little way to their right a light suddenly appeared, moving away from them.

Spot half turned to look at the children, as if he was about to warn them of something, but a moment later any such warning was too late.

With a savage growl a dog sprang out of the undergrowth and landed on Spot. At once the shape of the two dogs turned into a madly twisting mass of fur and claws as they fought for supremacy. Spot's agitated barking mingled with the vicious snarling of his opponent.

'Spot!' Alice hissed, scrambling up the hill

towards them. But William grabbed at her, putting a hand over her mouth.

'Stop, Al! You can't help him,' he whispered. 'You'll get torn to pieces if you try to separate them now.'

Alice fought him with her clenched fists, hitting at his face and tearing at his hair in her anguish, but William had her securely.

Out of the shadows up above them the figure of a man appeared. As he did so, he switched on a torch. The heaving, snarling mass of the two dogs leapt into view.

'Fang!' the man snarled.

It was a chilling sound, powerful and commanding. But still the dogs continued to fight.

'Fang! Drop!' the man shouted. 'Drop, I say!'

'What's to do?' the other man called and a moment later a second figure appeared beside the first.

'Fang! Here, dog. Come here!'

With a final, ferocious yelp the seething mass separated once more into two dogs and one of them crept away up the bank towards the men.

'Come here, Fang!' the voice said.

The children dropped and pressed themselves against the thick grass of the hillside. Above them, Spot rose and limped away into the undergrowth. As he did so, the pinprick beam of light from the men's torch followed his movements.

'Dog, was it?'

'Looks like it.'

'Anyone with it?'

'Not sure.'

The light swung back, combing the rough

ground, getting nearer and nearer to where the children were hiding. Then, just when it seemed inevitable that they would be discovered, another voice, a woman's, rang out from the top of the hill.

'You, down there!' it called. 'I can see you. I have informed the police that you're here . . . '

'Scarper!' one of the men hissed and they disappeared along the lower ridge and into the trees. As they went, one of them called in a low, hoarse whisper:

'Fang!'

17
The Sett

'Now, Gypsy,' Meg Lewis said, stroking Spot's head, 'let's have a look.'

The dog lay on his side and allowed her to peer at his neck.

'Could one of you hold the torch?' she asked, after a moment.

Alice reached across and took it from her.

'Just point the light here, pet. That's fine. Now, let's see what the damage is. Oh, my poor! Oh, my beauty!' Meg sang the words in a gentle way, almost as a lullaby. Spot sighed and stretched and seemed unconcerned as he allowed her to examine the wound on his neck.

'It's not too bad, I think,' Meg told him. 'But you were lucky, mind. You should have known better. That was a vicious animal.'

'He didn't have any choice,' Alice immediately leapt to the dog's defence. 'The other one just came out of the dark and went for him.'

'Should be put down, a dog like that,' William muttered.

'No, pet!' Meg protested, gently.

'It just went for Spot,' William told her. 'He

hadn't done anything. It just attacked for no reason at all. Horrible thug!'

'Ah, but you see . . . ' Meg said, quietly, 'an animal is what his master has made him. In the wild, they only attack for survival. But that one has been trained differently. It's the master is the thug, pet. He's the one should be put away – not the dog.'

As she spoke, she produced a tube of ointment from her pocket and, squeezing a little on to her finger, she rubbed it on Spot's neck.

'D'you know who they were?' Mary asked.

Meg shook her head.

'I told you when we last met, it's only just started up again. I haven't had chance to find out much, yet. There pet,' she said to Spot, 'you'll soon heal.'

They were sitting on the grass at the top of the cliff not far from the yew tree. The night pressed in all around them. Dark clouds scudded across a star-lit sky. A breeze was stirring the branches of the trees. Distantly, a dog barked, making Spot raise his head, his nostrils quivering, his ears pricking forward, listening.

As the children stretched out on the grass, Mary put her cheek against the ground and felt the cool damp of the dew.

Meg sat beside them, with her legs tucked up under her, leaning on one arm, watching the shadows.

'I was up in the hide,' she explained. 'I can keep an eye on the whole length of the sett from up there.'

'What's a sett?' Alice asked, turning on her side to look at Meg.

'Where badgers alive,' Meg explained. 'There's something big on. I heard from a friend across country. He came to see me. He thinks there's a meeting being organised.'

'A meeting?' William asked.

'You know – like you have a cricket match, or a horse race say,' Meg said. 'Well, the baiters get together and indulge in their sport as well. They choose a secret place, somewhere where they won't be discovered . . . '

'Then what? What do they do there?' Alice asked, dreading the reply. 'They don't race the badgers, do they?'

'Race them?' Meg exclaimed. 'No, pet. No! I told you before. They might bring four or five badgers to a meeting. Then they'll set the dogs on them, one after another. They put money on the dogs . . . bet which one will make the first kill; which one will kill the most; which one will last the longest in the ring . . . that's their sport, you see.'

'You mean the dogs . . . kill the badgers?' Alice asked.

'Eventually. Not too soon, they hope. That'd spoil their fun. But eventually the badgers die, yes. Sometimes the men do the killing themselves. A badger can put up quite a fight. Sometimes . . . if they get a really strong one, then he might be a match for the dogs – might look as if he's going to win. Then, as like as not, the men will impose a handicap.'

'What's that?' Alice asked.

'Well, you see, the baiters value their dogs, so

they don't want too much harm to come to them. If the badger looks as if it's going to win, they make it impossible for it to do so. They might muzzle it, or break one of its legs first . . . to give the dogs a better chance . . . ' She was silent for a moment, lost in thought, or perhaps in some terrible memory. Then she shook her head. 'Another favourite game of theirs is to tie the badger to a stake and set several dogs on it, all at the same time . . . '

'Oh, stop – please!' Alice said, covering her ears with her hands. 'Please don't tell us any more.'

'Bless you, child!' Meg said, putting an arm round her. 'I didn't mean to upset you. I thought you'd know these things.'

'How could we?' Alice sobbed. 'I've never even seen a badger, till I came here.'

'And it was dead,' Mary said, quietly, remembering Brock on the Dark and Dreadful path.

'Would you like to meet them? My badgers?' Meg asked and, as she spoke, she struggled to her feet. 'You stay here, Gypsy. Stay now.'

Spot looked up at her and wagged his tail.

'Better not have him along,' Meg explained. 'They might smell the blood and sense the fear. Come on then.'

As she led them over the edge of the cliff and down a steep narrow path, the moon came out from behind clouds and somewhere near at hand an owl hooted.

Mary looked up, searching the sky.

'Jasper!' she called, quietly.

Meg glanced back at her, a surprised expression on her face. Mary smiled, shyly.

'I have an owl that's a friend,' she explained.

'Only I haven't seen him since we've been here this time.'

'You're strange ones,' Meg said. 'You have owls and kestrels for friends. I think my badgers will take to you at once,' and, putting a finger to her lips, she motioned them to sit down on the grass.

For a while nothing happened and Alice began to feel sleepy. Then, just as she was about to suggest that maybe they should go home to bed, a movement further down the steep bank attracted her attention.

'Betty!' Meg whispered. 'Come on, my girl. Come and see.' And, rummaging in her pockets, she produced a handful of dried fruit.

'Raisins,' she whispered. 'Badgers love raisins!'

As the children stared through the half-darkness, the sweep of the ground below them was disturbed by what looked like a moving mound of earth. Gradually the mound resolved into a snout and the snout was followed by a long body, as a badger emerged from its underground den on to the moonlit turf. It sniffed the air cautiously and turned, rising up on its hind legs, to stare up the slope in their direction.

'Betty!' Meg called again, in the same singsong voice that she'd used with Spot.

The badger shambled up the hill towards them, stopping every few steps to sniff the air. When it reached where Meg sat, leaning forward, her hand outstretched with the raisins in her palm, it reared up once more and put both its front paws on her shoulders. A pungent, acrid smell filled the air.

'She's musking me,' Meg explained in a whisper. 'Aren't you, my girl? It's her way of welcoming me. Here,' and she held out her hand again and the badger licked off the raisins.

Now other badgers started to appear from several different, well-concealed, holes. At first they were tentative because of the presence of the children. But, in time, they became more relaxed and took raisins from their outstretched hands and one of the smallest, whom Meg introduced as . . .

'Candy. She's from Stella's last litter . . .'

. . . actually came and nuzzled up to Alice and, to her delight, fell asleep in her lap.

Meg knew all the badgers by name. There was Trish and Grey and all the cubs and a big male called Bawson. Bawson kept himself apart from the others. He stood, raised up on his haunches, with his head moving from side to side, listening for sounds of danger.

'They still miss Brock,' Meg explained, sadly. 'Poor Brock. He was the leader. Now Bawson has the responsibility.'

The smell of badger was strong on the air and the sound of their breathing and snorting, as they rooted in the undergrowth, foraging for food, was so foreign to the children that it seemed like a dream they were living and that soon they would wake up and find themselves in bed, as Alice had woken from the flight with the swallows.

'These are my badgers,' Meg whispered. 'These are my friends. They have no enemies in the wild world, except only men. Men, like those two, who kill them for sport. Can you explain that to me? Can anyone explain it? Isn't that the most horrible, saddest, thing you ever did hear? Look at them. Creatures of the night, family animals, with aunts and uncles and grannies, who live together in a close-knit group, caring for each other, grieving for each other – and men like that will come with dogs that they have bred specially to be vicious killers. They'll rip open the setts and they'll take the badgers and then they'll enjoy watching these beautiful, peaceful, loving creatures being torn to pieces. Why? What has become of us? How can it be that some of us – flesh of our flesh – can be like that? How?'

As she spoke, the badgers crowded round her, rubbing themselves against her, playfully batting her with their paws and ruffling her hair with their snouts until, at last, they reduced her to troubled silence.

A long time later she said:

'I never have understood that. That's why I don't mix with people. I like it here, in the night, with my friends.'

Eventually it was time for the children to go. The first glimmer of dawn was showing in the eastern sky and an early blackbird began to sing.

'How will I keep them safe,' Meg whispered as they were preparing to leave, 'with these men about? These lampers and baiters . . . ?'

'You said the police were coming,' Mary said. 'Was it true?'

Meg shook her head.

'It is sometimes. They're very good. But it's a long way out here from the town. I said it to scare the men off. The police came last time. That's how we stopped it then. There's one man, he's a sergeant now, Bob Parker, he cares about the badgers. He'll always come if I can get hold of him. But I don't have a telephone. He comes round to see me sometimes. But it's luck if he's here on the right night. We have to know in advance, what's going on. We need to know who those men are. We must always try to be one jump ahead of them.'

'We can find out who they are,' William said, suddenly.

'You can?' Meg asked, surprised.

'They gave themselves away,' William told her.

'How?'

'One of them called his dog Fang. We've come across that name.'

'And the dog as well, William. We've seen that dog before,' Mary added, grimly.

'Are you sure?' Meg asked.

'Oh, yes. I'm certain,' Mary told her. 'That dog belongs to one of the builders working on Uncle Jack's house.'

'From Golden House,' Meg whispered. 'Nothing but trouble ever comes from Golden House.'

'What can we do to help?' William asked.

'If you really know this man, then maybe there is hope,' Meg told them. 'Come and see me at Four Fields as soon as you're able.'

They promised they would and said that they'd bring Uncle Jack with them.

'He'll help,' Alice told Meg. 'He'll stop the awful men.'

The children collected Spot from the crest of the hill and, leaving Meg still surrounded by the badgers, they hurried down the steep side of the valley through the growing morning light. Then Mary suddenly stopped in her tracks. 'Oh!' she exclaimed.

'What, Mare?' Alice asked.

'If that horrible dog does belong to Kev, the builder, you know what else it means?'

'I think I do, yes,' William said, quietly.

'It means it was Kev who wrote on the floor in the crypt and . . . '

'It was Kev who wrote on the mirror in the secret room,' Alice whispered. 'Kev has discovered the Magician's room. Oh, William, Mary – what should we do?'

'We'll have to ask the Magician,' William said, emphatically.

'But how?' Mary asked. 'He's never there when we need him.'

'We'll have to, somehow, contact him,' William said.

'But how, William?' Mary repeated.

'I don't know,' he answered in a forlorn voice.

'It'll be all right,' Alice said. 'I know it will,' and she hurried ahead, with Spot limping beside her.

18
The Alchemy Begins
To Work

The children didn't manage to get up to the secret room until late in the afternoon of the following day. Arthur and Dan continued to plaster in the Tudor wing and Kev, once he had finished clearing the heavy stuff from the cellars, was sent to join them.

'He's no good at plastering,' Arthur confided in Jack in a mournful voice. 'But I expect we can find something for him to do. He's not bright, but he is strong and that can come in very handy in the building trade.'

During the morning the children and Spot were crossing the yard when they came face to face with Kev, who was sitting on the back of the truck with his dog, smoking a cigarette.

'Yours been in a scrap, has he?' Kev asked, nodding in the direction of Spot. He climbed down off the van, obviously embarrassed to have been caught not working.

'Why would you think that?' Mary asked, a defiant note in her voice.

'I just thought . . . he's got a nick on his neck.

Here boy, come and show me,' he said and he held out his hand to Spot, who backed away, growling and slunk off to the far side of the yard. 'You should train him,' Kev said. 'A dog needs to know who's boss.'

'He's very well behaved,' Alice said. 'He always comes when he's called.'

'There's more tricks than that you can teach 'em,' Kev told her. 'Wonderful obedient beasts. You can get them to do just what you want if you're firm with them.' As he spoke, he lifted his hand to his dog, making it shy away, cowering back in the van, its tail bewteen its legs. 'Look at that!' he said, proudly. 'I'll train yours if you like.'

'We don't want our dog to do tricks,' Alice said, turning her back.

'What's your dog called?' William asked.

Kev stared at him closely, then he grinned.

'Rover,' he replied and he went in to start work without another word.

'Rover!' William repeated, quietly. 'I bet he's got another name when he's working. Hey!,' he called, turning to look at the dog. 'Fang! Come on, Fang!'

The dog surged forward barking and growling, stopped from jumping at William only by the bit of rope round its neck. Even so, the immense strength of the dog was alarming and William took a step backwards.

'Oh, it's really frightening!' Mary said, retreating to the kitchen door.

'It's the man's fault,' Alice said. 'I feel almost sorry for the dog.' But she hurried into the kitchen all the same, wanting to get away from the snapping and growling.

The children continued to help clear the cellars with Jack. Then, when all the disposable stuff had been removed and the rest was stacked neatly in piles, they swept out the rooms and brushed down the walls, removing cobwebs and layers of grime as they did so.

When the yard was empty, Spot returned and sniffed round the van. Whatever he discovered there made him growl again and Phoebe, who happened to be in the kitchen, making drinks for them all, called to him to come in and stop the noise.

During the afternoon, a lorry came and took away the skip, which was piled high with rubbish. Then Jack told the children to have a break.

'Get some fresh air,' he said. 'I really didn't mean you to spend the holiday working.'

As soon as they were alone, they went up to the secret room. They were so used to the steps up the chimney by now that they didn't bother to bring a torch.

William opened the shutters on both the windows and the light filtered in revealing the dusty, empty space and the dark, cobwebby corners.

'Now what?' Mary asked. 'How do we get the Magician to come?'

'Maybe if we all think about him really hard,' William suggested.

But that didn't work at all.

'I find it quite hard, just thinking about him,' Mary observed. 'I mean, are we supposed to think about how he looks, or his voice, or what he says . . . or, what? I mean, how do you think about something?'

'I meant concentrate,' William said, sounding irritable.

'I know what Mary means, though,' Alice cut in. 'I keep thinking about something else all the time, like food or that time Phoebe took her boob out and fed the baby.'

'Shut up, Alice,' William said, squeezing his eyes closed and saying the Magician's name over and over in his mind.

'I think if we imagined him here, that might work better,' Alice suggested.

But imagining turned out to be as difficult as thinking and in a short while they were all bored. Mary got up from the floor where she'd been sitting cross-legged and sauntered over to the corner where the mirror was fixed to the wall.

'You're so vain, Mare,' Alice said, not hiding her disgust.

But Mary didn't rise to the bait. She stood for a moment, silently staring at the mirror, then, without looking round, she said:

'Come and look. There's one of those funny drawings on it this time.'

William and Alice hurried over to join her. She was right. Dimly, in the fine dust that covered the surface of the glass, they could just make out a crude drawing of a sun and a moon, divided by a single line.

'It's another of those symbols,' William said, speaking to himself. 'But who put it there, and why?'

'Well, it wasn't there when I came up here,'

Alice said and then she started to blush as the other two turned on her.

'Did you come up here on your own, Al?' William demanded, sounding fierce.

'I was going to tell you,' Alice said, in a small voice.

'We have a Solemn Vow, Alice,' William shouted, immediately losing his temper.

'Keep your voice down,' Mary hissed. 'And anyway, I don't see how you can be so cross, William. You broke the Solemn Vow twice at Christmas.'

'It isn't safe for her, coming on her own,' William insisted.

'Well, what else was I supposed to do?' Alice demanded, losing her temper as well. 'You were both mooching around. We weren't getting anywhere.'

'Oh, shut up, both of you,' Mary interjected. 'Losing your temper won't help. Did you draw this on the mirror, Alice?'

'No, of course I didn't. I expect it was Mr Tyler . . . '

'That's it!' William exclaimed. 'Of course. The Magician more or less told us.'

'Oh, William – what?' Mary said, losing her patience.

'This mirror is somehow special – don't you remember? He said in his time it isn't this shape – but the other way round, like a bowl . . . '

'So?' Mary demanded.

'I don't know. Maybe if we . . . use the mirror . . . If we all . . . stare at it and . . . maybe,

175

if we try not to think of anything, but just concentrate on it . . . '

Mary produced a handkerchief out of her jeans pocket and dusted the glass, trying to remove the drawing.

'That's odd,' she said. 'It won't come off.'

'Let me see, Mare,' William said, taking the handkerchief and wiping the mirror.

But Mary was right. There was no dust on the surface of the glass and the drawing remained however much he rubbed.

'I can't move it,' he said. Then, looking round at the girls with a troubled expression on his face, he added, 'It's almost as though it's drawn on the other side.'

'What d'you mean?' Alice asked, alarmed.

'As though, somehow, the drawing is on the inner surface of the glass,' William replied, thoughtfully.

The three children stood in a row, staring at the mirror. At first they could see their own faces gazing back at them, the image slightly distorted by the rounded glass, with behind and around them the dusty, empty room. Then, very gradually, their reflections started to fade.

'Oh!' Alice gasped.

'Sssh!' William hissed.

'But, we're disappearing,' Alice whispered.

As she spoke, their three faces came back into sharper focus.

'Alice!' Mary cried.

'What?' Alice cried.

'You've stopped it,' Mary said.

It was true. The reflection of their three faces was returning to normal.

'It wasn't me. Why are you blaming me?'

'You shouldn't have talked,' William snapped.

'But . . . it was so . . . ghosty.'

'The drawing is still there,' Mary said.

'No, wait a minute,' William exclaimed and, taking the handkerchief he wiped the glass and, as he did so, the drawing was wiped away.

'It's on this side of the glass now. But . . . how? I don't understand. It wasn't before. What does it mean?'

'It means,' a voice behind them announced, 'that you have come close to time travelling. And I am very, very impressed.'

19
Alice Loses Her Temper

Stephen Tyler was standing by the front window, leaning with one hand on the sill and holding his silver stick in the other. He nodded, gravely, as they turned to look at him.

'You're here!' Alice exclaimed with delight. 'We made you come!'

'You most certainly did not!' he retorted. 'I am not at your beck and call! But you have achieved a small degree of expertise. And that is most reassuring. Do you know how you did it?' he asked them.

The children all shook their heads.

'That's a pity. An ignorant skill is a useless gift,' Stephen Tyler sounded disappointed. 'It simply means that what you have achieved took place by accident. One cannot rely on it. And yet there was some reasoning there. You, William, tell me what you think happened.'

'We all wanted you to appear so much that we . . . sort of willed you to,' William stammered, uncertainly.

'Willed? I'm not sure about that. It takes a powerful mind to employ the Will. Mary?'

Mary shrugged and blushed.

'We just imagined you here . . . '

'No we didn't, Mary,' Alice interrupted her. 'I suggested that but we gave up because we couldn't do it properly. Actually I wasn't thinking of anything in particular when our faces started to disappear. I was just sort of . . . at a loss.'

'Good,' the Magician said, nodding enthusiastically. 'Very good! Let me tell you about the first stage in the making of gold . . . True gold; the Philosopher's Gold. The stage is very simple. You take a pound of mercury and heat it in a crucible until it begins to smoke. That is all. Mercury . . . quicksilver . . . that substance that runs hither and thither and is never still.' He stared at them with his piercing eyes. 'Listen to me, my pupils. Mercury is the mind. All you must do, to take the first step on the journey to becoming gold, is to stop the mind from buzzing here and there, pursuing every little thought that enters the head, every little idea, every little craving or sensation. Stop the mind . . . and hold it still. Is that all, you may ask? Believe me it is the hardest bit of the whole process. To still the mind takes years of practice usually. You are doing very, very well. I am pleased. Now, the next stage is, little by little, to warm the Mercury; to warm the Mind. With what should you warm it? Hmm? Is that what you ask? I will tell you a great secret.' He lowered his voice. 'The only way to warm the mind is with the heat of the heart.' He turned and looked out of the window. 'So – shall we start the next stage at once? It is a hard one. Are you ready for it?' He turned and looked at them again. 'Perhaps,' he murmured quietly. 'Very well . . .' and his voice changed to a bright and cheerful tone. 'Ask me some questions now!'

The children all started speaking at once. There were so many questions that needed to be answered.

'Has Kev found the secret room?' William demanded.

'Ask him,' he was advised.

'But, if he has . . .'

'It will mean nothing to him. All he will have found will be an empty room at the top of the house.'

'With steps that go down the chimney. Won't he think that a bit odd?'

'He will mistake them for the steps of the old tower and he will find the way blocked half way down with the wooden smoke door. I repeat – it will not mean a thing to him. A blocked up attic room and half an ancient staircase. Trust me. People who lack imagination see only what they think is in front of them.'

'But . . . you said it disturbed you, people coming in here.'

'Did I? Perhaps. But not in your time. In my time it disturbs me a great deal. Remember that, if you ever come to visit me.'

'That's hardly likely, is it?' William said, grumpily.

'I would have thought it extremely likely. You are all doing very well. But don't concern yourself with the future. That is one of the mind's favourite tricks – it runs off into the future or into the past, and it is rarely if ever, here, in the present moment

– now! As for this man . . . just ask him and see what he says. Questions?'

'How does the drawing on the mirror work?' Mary said quickly, not wanting William to hog all the attention.

'Presumably this . . . Kev . . . wrote the strange message. OK?' Stephen Tyler said, with a smile, and sounding as if he was using a well-rehearsed phrase from a foreign language he was learning.

'No!' Mary insisted. 'You don't understand. There was something new. Here, today.'

'Tell me,' the Magician said.

Again they all started talking at once, explaining to Stephen Tyler what had happened. The room was full of their chattering voices.

'Stop!' he cried. 'You're like a lot of hens. Hens do not make good pupils!'

Mary was chosen to explain what had occurred because she had asked the original question. Stephen Tyler listened, quietly, to her story.

'This is very interesting,' he observed at last. 'The mirror, as you call it and as I think I have explained before, is in truth the Philosopher's Glass in my study. It is used for a great variety of things, but mainly as an aid to contemplation. Sometimes, for increased awareness, I sketch symbols on the glass with my fingers. It started off, you say, on my side of the glass – as it were – and ended up on yours . . . ' He nodded to himself, thinking deeply. 'I think this confirms that, for a moment, you all were there . . . in my time. And, when you returned, you were concentrating so hard on the symbol that you . . . brought it with you.' He paused, considering. 'But who drew the symbol?' he said at last. 'That is quite another question. It could only have been me – and I certainly didn't – or . . . Morden. Morden!' He repeated the name, his voice rising angrily. 'That meddlesome assistant!' and he paced the room, shaking his head and lost in thought again.

'If he's so much trouble,' Mary exclaimed, 'you should get rid of him.'

'No, no!' the old man muttered, calming down a little. 'I can't. I also am on this journey, you know. I also hope to be transformed. To make gold it is necessary to employ dross. You cannot get the one without the other. Morden is my dross. Besides, without his sobering influence, I would be in danger of becoming complacent. He is useful to my endeavours because he makes me work harder. Morden is my conscience, my timepiece. He reminds me of how much there is still to do, he keeps me at it. I always need to be one step ahead of Morden. A Magician who works with angels, must have a close knowledge of devils.'

'Oh, please!' Alice exclaimed, desperately. 'Just tell us one thing . . .'

'And what is that, Alice?' Stephen Tyler asked her, staring coldly.

'How can we help the badgers?' she demanded.

'The badgers?' the Magician said. 'Why are badgers important?'

'Why?' Alice exclaimed. 'The badgers are being killed . . .'

The Magician stared at her thoughtfully for a moment and, when he next spoke, his mood had changed. His eyes flashed and his voice was angry.

'Little girl,' he said, 'we are here to discuss the transformation of your mortal soul and you bother me with badgers?'

'You told us to care about them,' Alice retored indignantly,' and besides they've never done any harm to anyone. Meg says they haven't any enemies except the men. They kill them . . . for fun . . . '

'But, Alice,' Stephen Tyler said, more gently, 'nature has ever been cruel. We cannot change that.' As he spoke he held out his hand, as if inviting her to move closer to him. 'Come,' he whispered, 'we have much more important work to do. Don't bother your head with this.'

Alice looked at him with sudden disgust. She saw an old man in a long black cloak, with thin wisps of red hair round his nearly bald head. He didn't seem magical any more, just ordinary.

'More important? There isn't anything more important,' she cried. 'If you can't see that then . . . you're almost as bad as they are. We thought you'd help us.' She felt a lump swelling in her throat and swallowed hard, willing herself not to cry. 'I thought you wanted us to understand about nature and things. Well, the badgers are nature, aren't they?'

'You're wasting my time,' Stephen Tyler rapped, raising his silver cane, threateningly.

'I'm going to help the badgers,' Alice said defiantly.

'You will put me in a fury.'

'Good!' she shouted. 'I don't care . . . '

'Alice,' Mary whispered, warningly.

'No, Mare. You can't stop me. I don't care what he does. I don't care if I never see him again.

I don't care if I never come up here again. I don't
care about anything – the magic or anything. If he
can't see that the life of the badgers is as important
as his silly alchy-thing, then I don't want to know
about him. I shall go to see Meg Lewis in future.'
She turned and faced the Magician once more, her
face flushed with anger, her whole body shaking. 'I
was the one who really believed in you. I was the
one who never stopped thinking about you and
couldn't wait to get back here. I can't believe that
you won't help us . . . ' and, as she turned to run
out of the room and down the steps, the tears that
she had been holding at bay started to run out of
her eyes and down her cheeks.

After she'd gone, Mary and William glanced
at one another. They each hoped the other would
speak and were too afraid to do so themselves. The
Magician strode past them and went out on to the
landing.

'You will be on your own,' he shouted. 'I will
not be there to help you. There will be . . . NO
MAGIC.' He said the words with such force that
they echoed down the long stone stairwell.

'I don't care,' Alice's voice came back to him
from the dark, full of tears and pain.

Stephen Tyler returned. He was so angry that
his eyes blazed like coals.

'She will be made to care. And you
two . . . What have you to say to me? Will you also
defy me? Will you also behave in this hysterical,
sentimental way? Will you also turn your backs on
the great work – for the sake of a few animals? Well,
one of you speak.'

'Come on, Will,' Mary said, holding out her

hand nervously to her brother. 'We have to go now,' she continued, edging past the Magician.

'Go? Where?' he thundered.

'With Alice,' William replied, in an unsteady voice.

'Stay here,' the Magician commanded. 'I have work for you to do.'

'I'm sorry, we have to go,' William repeated, nervously.

'I will really lose my temper,' the Magician raged.

Mary had reached the door. Now was the moment to make her escape. William was just behind her. Together they could run from the room. But something stopped her. There was something she had to say.

'I think Alice is right,' she said, turning. Then she hurried to continue before he could interrupt her. 'We don't understand what you want or anything. But, at least we understand the badgers. They're going to be killed for sport – like elephants and tigers and . . . all the other creatures; the whales and the dolphins, the wild flowers, the water we drink, the air we breathe. We're killing our world. Soon there won't be any animals left, if someone doesn't do something. Maybe it isn't like that in your time. Maybe you can't understand. Well, I'm very sorry, I'm with Alice. She's right. There's far more important work to do than your . . . alchemy-thing. It's right here, in this valley now. And I'm not sorry she said what she did. We thought you were our . . . friend. We thought . . . oh, come on, Will . . . ' and she dashed out of the room.

William turned and looked at Stephen Tyler. They stared at each other across the empty, dusty, unmagical attic.

'You as well?' the Magician asked, quietly.

William shrugged, uncertainly.

'I think you should have listened to Al,' he said. 'It is awful what's being done to the badgers.'

'Get out of my sight,' the Magician bellowed and, as William disappeared on to the dark landing, he shouted after him, 'I warn you, there will be no magic. You are all on your own now.'

The sound of William's footsteps echoed down the stairs. Stephen Tyler took a pace towards the door, then he stopped.

He smiled and nodded and, walking to the back window, he called quietly:

'Jasper, my bird. Come to me, Jasper.'

The creaking of wings heralded the arrival of a huge owl. It lighted on the sill of the window, blinking its great eyes and settling its wing feathers.

'Bring me Cinnabar, the fox and Sirius, the dog – there is work to be done. Meet me at the tree house. Warn Falco, the kestrel. Summon Merula, the blackbird. Tell the Swallows and the Swifts . . . I was right, my bird. Now it can begin . . .'

20
Four Fields

They went to Four Fields on Saturday. Jack said that he was taking the weekend off as all sensible people did and that maybe they'd like to go out in the Land-Rover and have a picnic.

'Maybe we could go into Wales,' he suggested. 'The hills will be looking wonderful at the moment.'

But Alice persuaded him that it was silly going somewhere else when they hadn't even started to discover the country right on their own doorstep. And so they all set off soon after breakfast, with Phoebe carrying Stephanie in a sling and Jack and William taking it in turns to carry the picnic in a haversack. Spot, who had gone out early that morning, was nowhere to be found and so, much to Alice's disappointment, they had to set off without him.

'He's never in the house now,' she moaned. 'I think he's gone off me.'

'We might meet him on the way,' Phoebe said, to cheer her up.

'And, if not,' Jack told her, 'he'll pick up our scent. He's very clever at finding things.'

William was given the job of navigating. He led them up the steep side of the valley, following a narrow path that was marked on the map and which brought them out on to the heights above Golden House not far from the yew tree.

They then cut across open country, before entering the beech woods once more. The lake they had seen on their previous visit, glinted through the trees to their left. Birds sang and a warm breeze stirred through the branches. They walked at an easy pace through the sun-dappled woods until they reached a broad path that cut like a swathe through the forest.

'It's marked as a bridle-path,' William announced.

'How much further are we going?' Phoebe asked, hitching Stephanie higher on her chest. 'You're a little ton weight, that's what you are!' she said, giving the child a kiss.

'Shall I carry her?' Mary asked.

'No,' Phoebe protested. 'You don't want to be bothered . . .'

'I'd like to,' Mary told her.

'I think she'd be a bit heavy for you,' Phoebe said.

'If we just go up this track,' William announced, studying the map, 'we'll come to those fields.' He pointed them out to Jack as he spoke. 'I think that's where Meg Lewis lives.'

Jack was surprised that they had a friend in the forest and so, as they continued up the bridle-path, the children told him and Phoebe all they knew about Meg. But, when they came to the events of the night encounter with the lampers, William tried to avoid too many details. However, Alice, in her eagerness, got carried away and it became quite clear to anyone listening what had really taken place.

'Wait a minute,' Jack exclaimed, turning to look at the three children. 'Are you telling me that you were chasing about in the forest in the middle of the night?'

'Well, not exactly . . . ' William mumbled.

'Then what has been going on?' Jack asked, his voice growing more angry.

'It was . . . Well, we saw these lights and, heard dogs barking and . . . '

'And you went out? In the middle of the night? Into the forest? Alone?'

'No, we were all together, honestly we were, Uncle Jack,' Mary explained.

'I cannot believe what I'm hearing,' Jack thundered. 'Are you all mad? Or are you just fools? Haven't you got a brain between you? These men could be violent. They could have attacked you. They could have abducted you. They could have molested you . . . You can't be so thick that you don't know the dangers.'

The children hung their heads.

'Well? What have you got to say for yourselves.'

'Meg goes out on her own,' Alice said quietly.

'I don't care what your friend Meg does. That isn't the point. I want no more of this nonsense. Is that understood?'

'But, Uncle Jack,' Alice insisted. 'We can't just let the men kill the badgers. We have to do something.'

Phoebe put a hand on her shoulder, comforting her.

'I have heard about these baiters,' she said. 'I can't believe that they come here.'

'They do, though,' William said. 'Meg will tell you.'

'We must stop them, Jack,' Phoebe said.

'Yes,' Jack agreed, sounding less angry. 'But all the same, I will not have the children putting themselves into danger . . .'

'I don't suppose they will again,' Phoebe said. 'Don't be angry any more with them. Not today. Look! This is such a magical place. Let's just enjoy it. Please, Jack.'

As they were talking, they passed under great arches of beech, the boughs covered with bright green leaves and festooned with wild honeysuckle. The air was sweet with its scent.

Then William, who was a little way ahead, called out: 'Come and see!' and, when they reached him, they found the way barred by an old wooden gate. Beyond it, the country opened out into a meadow. The grass was sprinkled with buttercups and clover. Tall daisies nodded in the breeze and tiny jewel-coloured pansies pushed up through the green turf. The field was not large and was bounded by a hedge. On the other side, through a gate, two cows and a few sheep could be seen munching contentedly.

'This is it,' Alice exclaimed excitedly and she climbed the gate and jumped down into the meadow.

'Hang on a minute,' Jack said. 'It's probably private property.'

But Alice was already racing across the field.

'It's all right,' she called. 'It must be Four Fields. And, if it is, we've been invited.'

'Alice!' Jack yelled again. 'Come back!'

But she had already reached the far gate and, swinging it open, she disappeared from view.

'I'm sure it'll be all right, Jack,' Phoebe said, trying the gate herself. But it was padlocked with an old chain. 'We'll have to climb over,' she said. 'You go first, and I'll pass Steph over to you.'

By the time they had all reached the other gate, Alice was returning across the second field, surrounded by three black and white dogs, who barked and jumped and seemed to have become her instant friends.

'Look,' she called, when she saw them. 'They're all like Spot! But he isn't here. Neither is Meg. I knocked on the door . . . Oh, do come and look,' she continued, excitedly, and she turned and raced off again.

In one corner of this second meadow a small, derelict-looking cottage was just visible. It was so shrouded in honeysuckle and ivy and the ground in front of it was so overgrown with flowers and vegetables that, apart from a door and a small window, it was difficult at first to identify it as a building at all.

A white cat lay, stretched out, in the sun on the doorstep. It opened a sleepy eye as Alice approached and yawned indolently. She stepped over it and banged on the door with her fist. As she did so, it swung open and three more cats in a variety of colours scampered out and disappeared into the undergrowth.

'Hello?' Alice called, peering into the dark hall. 'Hello? Is anyone there? Hello? Meg?'

But no answering call came from within and it was obvious that the house was empty.

'She isn't here,' Alice said, unable to hide her disappointment, when the others arrived. 'All this way, and she isn't here.' And she kicked the ground in a disgruntled way.

'Never mind,' Phoebe told her. 'Perhaps if we have our picnic, she'll have returned by the time we're finished.'

They found a place at the corner of the field under the trees and spread out the contents of the haversack. Phoebe had packed tomatoes and spring onions and slices of cheese and onion tart wrapped up in greaseproof paper. There were hard-boiled eggs and a bag of crisp lettuce; apples and pears and a big bottle of her own, home-made lemonade.

'You'll have to wipe the top,' she said. 'I haven't brought mugs or anything.'

The cows came over to see what was going on and two lambs were so fearless that one of them allowed Alice to feed it bits of lettuce, until its mother called to it and it scampered back to her.

'This is bliss,' Jack said, stretching out.

'I've never known such fearless animals,' Phoebe remarked. She had unbuttoned the top of her dress and was feeding Stephanie.

Alice was getting used to the sight by now. 'I don't exactly like to watch, if you know what I mean,' she had told William and Mary, after one feeding session, when they'd reached the privacy of their rooms, 'but . . . well, it is a handy way of feeding a baby, isn't it? It saves you having to carry about extra things all the time . . . bottles and . . . you know what I mean. And it'd be an awful waste of all that milk. It's just . . . ' and she'd shuddered. 'I hope it never happens to me. I think boobs are grotesque. If I start to grow them, I shall roll on the ground until I squash them flat,' and she'd giggled so much at the thought that she'd given herself hiccups.

But now, particularly here in the country, it didn't seem quite so rude and so, while not actually wanting to watch, Alice didn't mind too much. In fact she was intrigued enough to ask, while keeping her eyes fixed on a distant tree in the opposite direction to where Phoebe was sitting; 'Doesn't that hurt, Phoebe?' And Phoebe had laughed and told her that, yes, sometimes it did! 'She can be very greedy. Like now, for instance!' she said, with a laugh. But she didn't seem to mind too much.

'I'd offer to help!' Jack said in a sleepy voice, 'but I don't seem to be any good at all in that department.'

'Uncle Jack! Don't be rude,' Alice screamed, hitting him. 'Men don't have boobs. I know that much!'

'Shut up, Al.' Mary said in a dreamy voice. She was lying on her back, looking up at the sky, and she wanted only to hear the birds and the buzzing insects and the quiet munching of the cows. 'Oh!' she sighed. 'I could stay here forever,' and she drifted off once more into a half sleep.

By the middle of the afternoon Meg still hadn't arrived and, eventually Phoebe suggested that they should start making their way back to Golden House. The air was turning chilly and the sun, that had been strong all day, kept disappearing behind clouds that had grown heavier and darker as time passed.

'Yes, we'd better get a move on,' Jack said, agreeing with her. 'It looks as if we'll be lucky to get home before the rain starts.'

They gathered up the debris of the picnic and put it back into the haversack.

'It's much lighter now, Will. Can you take it?' Jack asked. 'And I'll carry my daughter. Come on, sausage!' he said, picking Stephanie up and giving her a kiss.

'Uncle Jack!' Alice exclaimed. 'Please don't call her that. You'll make me miserable.'

'I meant a vegetarian sausage, of course!' Jack said, giving Phoebe a kiss on the cheek.

'Mmmh!' Phoebe said, playfully. 'You meat eaters. How would you like it if those two beautiful cows minced you up for breakfast?'

Put like that even Alice had to admit to a certain sympathy with Phoebe's vegetable-thinking. The cows in question were sitting under a distant tree now, their legs tucked up under them, chewing steadily.

'But sausages aren't animals,' she said. 'They're just . . . things you buy from the butcher.'

'Ah!' Phoebe said, 'but the butcher has to get them from somewhere, Alice.'

And Alice sighed, because she couldn't think of a good enough answer and, actually, if she was honest, she'd enjoyed her picnic so much that she hadn't thought of sausages once till then.

'I shall remember this place always,' Mary said, looking back, as they climbed over the gate.

194

'So will I, Mary,' Phoebe agreed. 'And our picnic here. It was like . . . being in another world. A safe place.'

As they started down the broad bridle-path, the first splashes of rain dripped from the branches above their heads.

'We're going to get wet, I'm afraid,' Jack said, covering Stephanie's head with his sweater.

The day grew steadily darker and, by the time they reached their turning through the beech woods, thunder was grumbling in the distance.

'We'll have to shelter somewhere, Jack,' Phoebe called.

'I know where,' Alice whispered to William. 'Can we take them to the tree house?'

'I don't see why not. What do you think, Mare?' William asked.

Mary sighed.

'We may as well,' she said. 'Now that we've fallen out with the Magician, there doesn't seem much point keeping his secrets, does there?' And all three of them became instantly sad, as they remembered what they had given up.

'But all the same,' Alice said, brightening. 'It was quite magic-like just being at Four Fields. I still think Meg is special.' Then she added, 'I bet Meg can do spells.' But she said it without too much conviction.

'Come on, kids,' Jack called. 'We must find a big tree to shelter under.'

'This way, Uncle Jack,' Mary answered, and she led the way across the open ground towards the yew.

21
The Storm Clouds Gather

As the rain lashed down around them, Phoebe, Jack and the children ran for the cover of the yew tree. Jack held Stephanie close to his chest, with his thick woollen sweater covering her head and shoulders. She had woken from a happy burbling slumber and was whimpering miserably.

'I don't think our daughter likes rain much!' he said with a laugh, as they all reached the shelter of the thick branches and pushed through into the dark interior.

'She hasn't got wet, has she?' Phoebe asked in a worried voice, as she reached out to take the child from him.

'No. The sweater took most of it.'

Under the tree it was quite dry. Phoebe sat down, with her back to the trunk, and cradled Stephanie in her arms. The thunder, which had been distant, rumbled more closely and a sudden wind sprang up. Jack and William peered out through the hanging branches at the pelting rain. It bounced up off the earth and made puddles in all the hollows.

Mary and Alice stamped their feet and shook themselves, trying to get dry.

'It shouldn't last long,' Jack said.

As he spoke a crack of thunder exploded above them and a livid flash of lightning turned the world momentarily to the colour of sulphur.

Jack whistled!

'That was close!' he said. 'It must be right over us. It blew up so quickly.'

More thunder crashed. It was so loud that it shook the tree and made the branches tremble. Phoebe put a hand over one of Stephanie's ears and pressed her head gently to her breast, rocking her and soothing her as she howled fearfully.

Alice crouched with her back to the trunk, next to them. She didn't like thunder much either and could have done with a bit of comfort herself. But she was trying hard to be brave, so she just pursed her lips and hummed quietly and tunelessly to give herself some courage.

Mary, meanwhile, ran her fingers through her short hair, combing it dry. When William cried out, as a stream of water found its way through the tangled branches and went straight down the neck of his shirt, she squealed and dodged away from him.

'Oh, William!' she gasped. 'You gave me a fright.'

'That rain is very cold,' he said, trying to wipe his back dry with his hand.

Then Phoebe looked up and stopped the comforting noises she was crooning to the baby.

'Listen!' she said, urgently.

197

Another crash of thunder reverberated round the valley, and more lightning crackled and flashed.

'Listen!' she said again and, as she spoke, she pressed Stephanie closer to her, muffling her cries a little.

'What?' Jack asked.

'I'm sure I heard . . .'

'Help!' a faint voice cried, seeming to come from somewhere above them. 'Can somebody, please . . . help me?'

'Did you hear?' Phoebe said, breathlessly.

'Yes,' Jack replied and he gazed up into the tree in a puzzled way.

'Come on,' Mary said, running to the trunk. 'Up here, Uncle Jack!' and, as she spoke, she started to climb the lower branches, on the other side of the trunk from where Phoebe and Alice were sitting. As she did so, Alice scrambled to her feet.

'Ah! Is this the tree house you told us about?' Jack asked.

'Just follow us,' William told him, 'You'll see,' and he started to climb after Alice, who was already following Mary up the tree.

'You'd better stay here,' he told Phoebe, 'we can't carry Steph up as well . . .'

'Help me, please . . .' the voice called again.

The higher they climbed, the more the tree shook in the wind. When they came to the iron ring, William had to hold on to Alice and practically pass her across the gap to Mary. Jack, of course, found the going much easier because of his height.

'How on earth did you discover this place?' he asked William, as he stepped across the gap with

198

the aid of the iron ring, and joined him on the platform.

'It was an accident, really,' William answered. 'It'd take a bit of explaining.' They edged their way to the overhanging branch and ducked under it. Here Jack's height started to be a disadvantage and when he finally followed the children into the tree house – gasping with surprise at the sight of it – he had to stoop low to avoid hitting his head on the door frame.

The house swayed and shook in the wind and the noise of it tearing at the open shutters, making them bang and swing, was how it must be in the crow's nest of a ship in a gale. The space inside the room was limited and with them all there it was difficult to move. Mary, ahead of the others, knelt down and only then were they able to see, over her, a figure lying on the floor. In the half light, it was just possible to make out a shock of white hair crammed under an old hat.

'Meg!' Mary cried. 'What's happened to you?'

'Oh, thank goodness you came, dear!' Meg exclaimed. 'I've been like this since the middle of last night. D'you think you could untie me?' And, as she spoke, she rolled over on her side, revealing that her arms and legs were tied securely behind her back in such a way that her legs were doubled under her.

'Let me, Mary,' Jack said and he squeezed past, producing a penknife from his pocket. With it he cut swiftly through the thick string, releasing her.

'You'll be the uncle, are you?' she said, squinting closely at him.

'Yes,' he said, 'I'm Jack Green. I live in Golden House. And you are . . . Meg?'

'Meg Lewis. That's right. Can you help me to stand up, please? I'm afraid I've been in one position for so long that I've got a bit stuck.'

'Who did this to you?' Jack asked, continuing to cut at the string.

'Who indeed. I didn't see the face, of course. Took me completely unawares. I'd just come here. The next thing I knew there was a gag in my mouth and I was being trussed up like a chicken. I managed to bite through the gag – but I couldn't get my hands or legs free.'

As she spoke, Jack cut the final pieces of knotted string from her ankles. There were dark red marks where it had bitten into her flesh. Meg massaged her wrists and ankles and stretched her limbs.

'You must be terribly shaken . . . ' Jack said, helping her to her feet. She stood, precariously, waiting for the circulation to return to her cramped body.

'Don't worry about me,' she said. 'It's the badgers who were in real danger,' Then she pushed past them, making for the door, and disappeared from view along the platform and under the branch.

Phoebe was standing at the foot of the tree, holding Stephanie and peering up, trying to make out what was going on. She was surprised when the first person who appeared, climbing rapidly and with great expertise down the trunk, turned out to be not one of the children or Jack but a little old lady in a long mac and a man's hat.

'Oh!' she exclaimed, as Meg pushed past her

without a word and went out, through the green screen of branches, into the still streaming rain.

A moment later, Jack appeared followed closely by William.

'Where is she?' Jack asked.

'She went that way . . . ' Phoebe replied, pointing vaguely in the direction that Meg had taken.

'Come on,' William said. 'I know where she'll have gone,' and he ran out into the rain.

Meg was kneeling in the mud, a little way down the steep side of the valley. The rain deluged round her, but she seemed not to notice it. When they reached her, she seemed equally unaware of their arrival. The ground around her was broken up and trampled – as though much digging had taken place. She held in her clenched hand a tuft of grey fur and, when she turned, her face was wet not just with the rain but with her own tears.

'Oh, my little ones! Oh, my dears! I've failed you,' she said, in a broken voice. 'I've failed you,' and then, unable to contain herself any longer, she leant forward on the wet earth, sobbing painfully.

Alice slid down the steep bank and, kneeling, she flung her arms round Meg hugging her close.

'Don't cry,' she whispered. 'Please don't cry, Meg. We know who one of the men is . . . '

'Too late, dearie. They've taken the badgers.'

'All of them?' Alice asked, appalled.

'No. They won't have bothered with the little ones or the old sows. I dread to think what's happened to them.' She wiped her cheeks with the back of a hand and, in doing so, smeared wet mud across her face. 'What beats me is – how did they know where I was?'

'Tell us what happened,' Jack said.

'I was up in the hide. I hadn't seen a sign of lamps.' She closed her eyes, trying to remember. 'There was a noise behind me. I looked round . . . it was dark, you see, and I never use a torch, for fear of giving myself away. Next thing I knew – someone jumped on me. I was gagged and trussed up before you could say "Hollyhocks".'

'How long had you been up there?'

'No time. I'd spent most of the night down here, at the sett. But the wind was cold and there didn't seem anyone about. Besides, I get a much better view from up there. I can see if anyone's coming from either direction. No, I'd scarcely climbed the tree and got myself settled when it happened.'

'So, whoever it was could have been watching you for quite some time and followed you up there?'

'Could have, I suppose,' Meg agreed, reluctantly. 'But I'm usually so alert. I'm used to the dark, see. It's no different from daylight for me . . . ' She fell silent again, stroking the tuft of fur in her hand.

'Come back under the tree, out of the rain,' Jack said, raising her up.

Mary and William were standing just behind her. Mary took her hand and helped her to climb back to the top of the bank. William, meanwhile, reached down and gave Alice a pull up.

'If only . . . ' she said, quietly.

'What?' he asked, half knowing what she was thinking.

'If only I hadn't lost my temper with the Magician. He'd be able to help us. I'm sure he

202

would too, if he knew what was going on. Don't you think so, Will . . . ?'

But William didn't respond and so they continued up the hill in silence. The rain was lighter now and the thunder sounded more distantly. When they reached the yew the others were preparing to leave.

'Come with us, Miss Lewis,' Phoebe was saying. 'We're much nearer to Golden House now than to your place and we can take you back in the Land-Rover . . . There is a road to you, is there?'

'Yes, dear,' Meg answered. 'There's a track through the forest, takes you out on to the moor road. I hardly ever use it now. I don't go to the town much. Don't really fit in there any more.'

'Please come with us,' Phoebe repeated, gently, and Stephanie reached out with her hands and stroked Meg's cheeks.

Meg smiled, sadly, and took the little fingers in her hand.

'A Lewis going back to that place?' she said to herself. 'Maybe the time has come. For my badgers at least.' She looked into Phoebe's eyes. 'For them, shall I forget the past? Forgive . . . and forget?'

Phoebe frowned, not understanding what Meg was talking about, but troubled none the less by her words.

'Do you hate our house so much?' she asked.

'Not the house itself, more what it does to people.'

'Come on,' Jack interrupted them, stopping any further conversation. 'We'd better hurry, while the rain has stopped.'

As they left the cover of the tree, Mary and

Alice ran to Meg, each taking one of her hands and drawing her along after them. Phoebe lifted Stephanie higher in her arms, covered her with Jack's sweater, and followed the others through the wet grass to the edge of the valley.

'Well, I mustn't be long,' Meg told the girls, still sounding unsure. 'There are the cows to milk . . . the animals will wonder where I've been.' Then a sudden thought made her look back towards the yews. 'Did you see Gypsy? I thought I heard him, not long after dawn. You'll know where he is if anyone does,' she added, turning to Alice.

'I haven't seen Spot for ages,' Alice replied, unable to call him by any other name. 'He's gone off me, I think.'

'Never, dear!' Meg told her. 'When you win the love of a dog, you win it for life. He's probably been a bit busy. The animals have a life to lead as well, you know. We don't know the half of what they get up to!'

'This way!' William called from ahead of them and he disappeared down the steep path.

Meg took a deep breath, as if steadying her nerves.

'So,' she said, 'it's come at last. A Lewis returns to Golden House.'

22
'A Lewis Returns to Golden House'

As soon as they arrived home, the children all went upstairs to change and Jack took Stephanie to their bedroom. Meanwhile Phoebe led Meg through the hall to the warmth of the kitchen.

'You're sure you wouldn't like something to change into yourself?' she asked. 'A dressing gown, perhaps?'

But Meg just shook her head and took off her raincoat.

'Thank you kindly, dear, but I'm more often damp than not, you know,' she told her, shyly. 'You can't help it when you live out of doors. I never notice the wet to tell the truth. It's all one with me, rain or fine.'

So Phoebe drew up one of the chairs to the kitchen range and left Meg warming herself, while she went up to put on a dry dress. When the children came down they found Meg sitting on the edge of the seat, staring into the flames.

'Funny, me being here,' she said, in a dreamy voice. 'Funny! My family used to own all this, you know. But my grandad lost it. Gambling. That's what I was told – that was his vice. He never seemed like a gambling man to me. 'Course I was only little when he died. He was a haunted man. We've all been haunted – by this place. Golden House!' she said the words with such bitterness. 'Golden House! It was ever gold that was man's undoing. I've never set foot inside the place till now, but I could tell you every corner of it. Every nook. Every cranny. I know about rooms here you'd never even dream existed. Grandfather Lewis spent all his days sketching maps and diagrams. I can see him now, poring over bits of paper, doing sums, rubbing out, starting again, throwing sheet after sheet of paper on the fire. All the time, shaking his head and muttering to himself. Poor man. This place destroyed him, yet – even after he got away – he couldn't let it alone. And my father too. The memory of it drove him into an early grave. Mother and I were left to fend for ourselves. And then, one day, I came home from the market – I'd been to sell a bull calf, I remember – and Mother had passed away as well; carried off by worry and a broken heart. And there I was, left alone at Four Fields, who should have been the mistress of all this.' She became silent again, staring into the glowing fire.

'D'you still have the sketch maps?' William asked her. 'The ones your grandfather did of the house.'

Meg looked at him, as if surprised not only by his question but that he was there at all, so lost had she been in her thoughts.

'What, dear?' she asked.

'Do you still have the maps that he did?'

'Yes and no,' she replied. 'I burnt them with all the other stuff – I sold what I could and burnt the rest. But you can't burn the memory, can you?' She tapped her forehead. 'I have them in here,' she said. 'Nice and safe in here. No one will get them out of me. Not ever. They destroyed him – I wouldn't want that to happen to someone else, would I? And have it be my fault.'

'D'you know about the room at the top of the chimney?' Alice whispered.

'I tell you,' Meg whispered back. 'I know everything.'

'And yet you've never been here?' Mary asked.

'Not in the flesh. But my mind has brought me here most days. The mind travels far swifter than the body. I sit in that tree house and stare at this place. I'm glad children are living here again. It needs laughter and warmth. It was a sad house when the Crawdens were here. He was a terrible cruel man. He drove my grandad and grandmother out for a debt of money, when he already had more than enough. My daddy was two years old at the time. But they had to get out, taking him – a little babe-in-arms – with them and nowhere but a poor tumbledown cottage in the middle of the forest to call their own. Hard times. Still, all things come to those who wait. Eventually the house became empty – that was after old Miss Crawden died – and we were the only two left in the valley, this house and me. I've watched it, day after day, slowly falling into ruin. It's what our family wished for, you see, that one day Golden House would be no more and that its power would . . . fail.'

'What power?' William whispered, as the children all sat, wide-eyed, listening to her.

'I think you know well enough what I'm talking about,' Meg said, looking at them.

'The Magician isn't really bad,' Alice said. 'Honestly, I'm sure he isn't. It's just that – he's a bit stern sometimes and he gets cross when we ask the wrong questions.'

'He destroyed my grandad,' Meg said, bitterly.

'But I think . . .' William told her, trying hard to remember, 'I think we read all about it in a book Uncle Jack brought back at Christmas. He'd borrowed it from some woman at the museum. Was your grandfather called Jonas Lewis?' Meg nodded. 'Then the book was written by him . . .'

'I know the book,' she said, briefly. 'It was ours once, but I sold it. I needed money to keep Mother and me alive and what did we need with a book full of Granda's blessed drawings? We'd seen enough of them over the years . . .'

'Well if you've read the book, you'll remember . . . it was because he'd made gold for his own use that the Magician was angry . . .'

'Yes. I remember,' Meg said, after a moment. 'I remember that story. But – just supposing it was true – would it have been such a crime? He'd used up every penny he had on those blessed experiments. Every penny. Need he have been so sorely punished for his deed? Wasn't the object to make gold? Poor man, didn't he suffer enough? Was there to be no forgiveness . . . ?'

The children felt uncomfortable and could think of nothing to say. Then Meg shook her head, changing the subject.

'So now . . . a young man and his wife have arrived at Golden House with their baby daughter and their nephew and nieces . . . and the house is coming alive again; recalled to life . . . and, for the first time ever, I've come inside . . .' she shivered, as though she was cold, and reached closer to the open grate.

When Phoebe came in, having changed her clothes, she found the children and Meg sitting in silence.

'Jack's just coming,' she said, crossing to the larder for milk, and a moment later he came in to the room, carrying Stephanie.

'Sorry,' he said, laying the baby down in her cot. 'She needed changing. I'm a dab hand with the nappies!'

Phoebe made hot chocolate for them all. Meg was anxious to be off, but they persuaded her to stay.

'We want to know about the badger baiters,' Phoebe said, cutting thick wedges of cherry cake.

So Meg told Jack and Phoebe all that she knew about the baiters, up until the present catastrophe.

'Those badgers that'll have survived will go to ground, I shouldn't wonder,' Meg said. 'I'll find out the real damage tonight.'

'You won't go there again tonight?' Phoebe asked her.

'To the sett?' Meg asked, surprised. 'But of course I will. It's my home. Besides, I must, dear,' she continued. 'I failed them. I have to make it up to them. Those that are left, that is.'

'Where will they have taken the others?' Jack asked her. 'Any idea?'

209

Meg shrugged.

'That's the problem, dear. It could be anywhere,' she replied. 'These people will travel right across the country for a meeting. You get them coming out of Wales and the Midlands; Somerset; the North Country. They're clever, you see. What they're doing is illegal, so they keep moving on, that way the police never have time to catch them. I heard from a friend. There's been a lot of digging recently in his area. He lives over near Oxford, on the Cotswolds. He came to see me earlier in the week, told me all about it. I took him to see my sett.' She shook her head. 'When there's digging, it usually means they're collecting badgers for a meeting.'

'It's obscene!' Phoebe protested. 'What sort of people do this? Who are they?'

'Well, one of them, apparently, is rebuilding Golden House for you,' Meg replied, not disguising her disgust.

'What?' Jack cried.

So the children were called upon to tell what they had discovered.

'Fang?' Jack exclaimed, when they came to that part of the story. 'I'm sure Kev's dog isn't called Fang!'

'What is it called then?' Alice demanded.

'I don't think I've ever heard him call it anything,' Jack said, nonplussed. 'I admit it's a bit of a thug – and I'm glad he keeps it tied up – but I'm sure Kev isn't a baiter. He's just . . . well, he's a bit rough, but I get on very well with him.'

'You get on well with everyone,' Phoebe exclaimed.

'These people don't advertise themselves, Mr Green,' Meg said. 'They'll probably seem perfectly ordinary to their neighbours.'

'Anyway,' William cut in, 'who else could have written that Fang message down in the cellar?'

'And the one up in the secret room,' Alice said, the words coming out before she could stop herself.

'Secret room?' Phoebe said, looking at her.

Alice hung her head and blushed.

'What secret room?' Jack demanded. 'What's all this about? William? You may as well tell us.'

'There's a room at the top of the house, under the roof, next to mine,' he mumbled.

'Oh,' Jack laughed. 'We know about that! The sealed-up attic above the Georgian wing? Obviously the chap who owned Golden House when the alterations were done decided he had enough attics and didn't need another one. But, you're right, Kev did discover the room – when he was tiling the roof. We're thinking of opening it out with a door through from your bedroom, William. There's no other way into it.' The children glanced at each other. 'Is there?' Jack added, seeing their looks.

'You leave that room alone,' Meg cut in.

'What do you know about it?' Jack asked.

'I know it was a room my Grandad feared. "The top and the bottom of the house" – that's what he said. "That's where the trouble comes from. The top and the bottom". And yet. . . . All the time he was an outcast from this place, he worked and worked at the little drawings. I think he regretted what had happened so much that it turned his mind. Poor man! Poor all of us.'

Phoebe crossed to the old woman and put an arm round her shoulder.

'Don't be sad,' she said. As she leant forward, the pendant that she was wearing caught the light of the fire. Meg, seeing it for the first time, pulled away from her.

'Where did you get that necklace, dear?' she asked.

Phoebe, surprised, put her hand up to her throat, feeling the little talisman on its gold chain.

'Jack found it here. He cleaned it and gave it to me last Christmas.' The golden sun and the silver moon glinted in their frame of dull red metal. 'I love it, I wear it all the time.'

'It's very nice,' Meg said, sullenly. 'And yet . . . '

'What?'

'It reminds me . . . ' Meg shook her head. 'I don't know. Too many memories. That's why I like it out there – in the woods, in the real world. That's why I love my badgers. They have no time for imagining, for remembering. They show me another way of living. An easier way? Perhaps. A more honest way? Certainly. And then the men come . . . and destroy all that . . . For sport?' She shook her head, fighting back tears.

'And we think Kev is one of these men?' Jack said thoughtfully. 'Then, what's to stop me going to see him, now? If as you say, Meg, they've captured some badgers for this horrible sport of theirs, well, they must have hidden them somewhere. If I could catch him with one . . . '

'They don't keep them long,' Meg interrupted him. 'They'll be having the meet . . . tonight, I should think. Saturday night. That's when they usually do it. But where? That's the question. Where are they going to hold the cursed thing . . . ?'

At that moment, the back door burst open, admitting a gust of cold damp evening air. The group round the range turned, shocked by this sudden disturbance. Standing in the opening was the bedraggled and almost unrecognizable figure of a dog. His fur was soaked and mud-caked; there were dark matted patches of blood round his throat and on his shoulders; his eyes were wild and he was growling fiercely.

'Spot?' Alice whispered, taking a step towards him. 'Spot . . . ? Oh Spot, what's happened to you?' and she ran towards him, her arms held wide.

The dog limped a few steps into the room, looking up at Alice with pleading eyes, then shaking with fatigue and still bleeding from several open wounds, he collapsed on the floor in front of her with a pitiful sigh.

'Spot, oh Spot!' Alice cried, kneeling beside him. 'Darling Spot . . . oh please,' she sobbed, 'can somebody help him?'

Meg rose and hurried forward. Phoebe crossed and knelt beside Alice, putting her arms round her, hugging her.

'What shall we do?' Jack asked Meg, allowing her at once to take command.

'Dog fight, by the look of it,' Meg said, inspecting the body. 'That's not like my Gypsy, not like our Spot.' As she spoke she gently stroked the dog's head. 'I'll need some warm water and a little salt, to clean the wounds,' she said, brusquely. 'And you,

Alice, you must sit with him while I cut away the fur to see what damage is done.'

Alice nodded and put her hand on the dog's head. Spot moved slightly and licked her.

'There,' Meg said. 'He's brave now.'

23
Jasper and Cinnabar

Meg patched the dog up as best she could. There were several long deep scratches on his shoulders and across his back – 'Caused by claws, I should think,' she muttered, as she gently sponged them with salt water – and a much worse area on the neck, where fur and flesh had been torn away, leaving an open, oozing wound.'You should take him to the vet in the morning, if this bite looks at all septic,' she added. Then she cradled Spot's head in her hands and looked lovingly into his eyes. 'It was a nasty fight, old Gypsy. I wonder what it was all about?'

Jack, meanwhile, was anxious to leave.

'I want to reach Kev's house before he sets off. If you're right and the meeting is set for tonight, then we may already be too late. He could have gone by now and we'd have no idea where. Wherever this horrible thing is to take place, it might be miles away from here.'

'It might, yes,' Meg said, as she scrambled into her mac. 'And yet again, it might be right here on our doorstep. I wish the dog could talk. I bet he could tell us a thing or two.'

Alice drew closer to Spot, putting her hand on

215

the top of his head, seeking comfort from him and wanting to give it to him at the same time. She felt a sudden, terrible, guilt. If only she hadn't fallen out with the Magician, she thought, she would be able to speak to Spot and he would be able to tell her precisely what had taken place. 'Oh!' she cried in her head, 'How stupid I was,' and the dog sighed – a long, trembling, weary sound – and stretched himself painfully.

'Can I come with you, Uncle Jack?' William asked.

'No, better not. It might get a bit rough.'

'Oh, Jack – you will be careful,' Phoebe pleaded. 'You're not a fighter . . . '

'What should I do, then? Turn my back and let the badgers be killed.'

Phoebe shook her head and was silent.

'You go to Bob Parker first, at the Police Station,' Meg advised. 'There's nothing like a police uniform to calm the situation.'

'I must come, Uncle Jack,' William pleaded. 'I know more about it than you. I can explain ever such a lot. Please.'

'Come on then,' Jack said, after a moment's delibertion. 'You'll be all right, won't you?' he added, speaking to Phoebe.

'Yes, of course. Go quickly,' she urged him.

'If you drop me off at my lane end,' Meg said, as they crossed the kitchen to the door, 'I'll get back to the beasts. Once I've milked – and fed the dogs and cats – I'll go to the sett.'

'I don't like to think of you going back there,' Phoebe said, as they went out into the yard.

'They won't come back,' Meg assured her.

216

'They've done their worst. But I must know how many have been taken and how the little ones are faring.'

'Can I go with Meg?' Mary asked.

'Oh, I don't know. Jack, what d'you think?'

'She'll be safe with me,' Meg said. 'And it would be a help . . . '

'Yes, all right. But – come on,' Jack urged. He looked up at the darkening sky. 'I don't know how we'll begin to find them once the dark sets in.'

Alice, meanwhile, stayed in the kitchen, sitting on the floor beside Spot's basket where he lay, licking his paws and panting as though he'd been running a race.

'Oh, Spot,' she whispered again, miserably. 'It's all my fault. If only I hadn't lost my temper. We need some magic now . . . and there isn't any.'

They heard the Land-Rover start up and drive out of the yard and, a moment later, Phoebe came back into the room.

'Where's Mary?' Alice asked.

'She's gone with Meg,' Phoebe replied. She crossed to the cot beside the fire and looked down at Stephanie. 'She's sleeping soundly,' she said, 'as if she hadn't a care in the world. Oh, Alice – isn't it all horrible?' and, to Alice's amazement and embarrassment, she put her hand to her lips, turned her back, and started to cry.

'I feel it's all our fault,' she said. 'It's one of our builders who's doing this. He probably didn't know Golden Valley existed until we invited him here. I knew he was no good. I knew it . . . ' she shook her head and wiped her eyes with the back of her hands.

'I think it's my fault,' Alice said, in a small voice.

'Of course it isn't,' Phoebe said, blowing her nose. 'Look at us both!' and she smiled. 'Real miseries.' She crossed to the window and looked out into the yard. The evening was heavy and overcast. Darkness was already blotting out the view.

'It's just occurred to me,' she said, still with her back to Alice. 'How could you know about the attic above the Georgian wing? There isn't a way up to it. Kev only discovered it when he was doing the roof. How did you know about it, Alice?'

Alice shrugged.

'Don't know,' she mumbled.

'Is it a secret?' Phoebe asked, turning to look at her.

Alice shrugged again. Phoebe frowned and walked back towards the range, holding her hands out to warm them.

'Have you been up there?' she asked. Still Alice remained silent. 'Won't you tell me?'

Alice shook her head.

'Oh, Alice!' Phoebe sighed. 'I only want to be your friend, you know. Why won't you let me be? It can't just be because I'm a vegetarian! D'you mean to say – if I stuffed you full of sausages all the time you'd like me? I think that's silly. Shall I make you something to eat now? Oh, say something, Alice!' she shouted the last words, then she shook her head again: 'There I go, you see, losing my temper! Sorry,' she said and, picking Stephanie up out of the cot, she crossed to the door into the hall. 'I'm going up to bath Steph. D'you want to come?' she said.

Alice shook her head. 'I'll stay with Spot,' she said in a quiet voice. Then, looking at Phoebe standing at the door, she saw how miserable she looked. 'Actually, Phoebe,' she added, 'I quite like your cooking and I don't mind not having meat, honestly I don't. It's just that we're not used to it and anyway, I feel so miserable, because . . . it is all my fault, what's happening to the badgers. I know it is. You see,' and she couldn't stop her voice shaking as she spoke, 'I lose my temper as well – just like you do . . . only this time it's really serious 'cause I lost it with . . . ' she shook her head. Now wasn't the time to try to explain to Phoebe about the Magician. She sighed. 'You see,' she continued in a whisper, 'usually I can speak to Spot . . . I know that sounds mad but, honestly, I can. It isn't exactly magic – it's just something that happens . . . only I can't do it now. And, if only I could, he'd be able to tell us exactly where Kev has taken the badgers . . . and we'd be able to save them . . . ' and the tears that she'd been fighting back started to flow and her sobbing prevented her saying any more.

Phoebe crossed quickly and put Stephanie back into the cot, then she went and knelt down on the floor in front of Alice and put her arms round her.

'Don't cry,' she told her gently. 'Please don't cry, Alice. It isn't your fault. In fact your tears are as important for the badgers as anything . . . because they show that you care.'

'No!' Alice sobbed. 'It isn't enough. We've got to help them.'

'But that's what Jack is trying to do – and

William – and Meg – and Mary – right now. We're all trying to help.'

As Phoebe held Alice and wiped the tears from her cheeks, Spot rose from his basket and came and sat in front of them both, staring solemnly up into Alice's face.

'Look at Spot,' Phoebe said, 'he can't bear to see you unhappy.'

'Oh, Spot!' Alice sighed, then, as she looked at him, she suddenly remembered the words the Magician had said to her when she had seen him alone in the secret room: 'Just be silent . . . Don't fight it, Alice . . . don't resist . . . just . . . imagine . . . ' and, as she remembered, so, for a moment, her mind was stilled.

'That's better,' Spot whispered in her head.

Alice gasped and looked quickly at Phoebe, wondering if she also had heard the words. But obviously she hadn't, because she continued to rock Alice gently and then she said:

'Come and help me bath Steph,' and she gave her an extra hug.

Alice shook her head, then, surprising even herself, she gave Phoebe a kiss on the cheek.

'I'm all right now. I'll stay here with Spot.'

'You're sure?' Phoebe asked and, when Alice nodded, she rose and went to collect Stephanie.

'And Phoebe . . . ' Alice added. 'Whatever I do, you won't be cross, will you? I mean . . . '

'Alice!' Phoebe cut in. 'I never mean to be cross. I hate it just as much as you do when it happens. But, try to understand – this is strange for me as well, you know. I'm not used to having children around. Or this little bundle of energy!' As she spoke she lifted Stephanie and gave her a kiss. 'When I'm cross, I'm usually being cross with myself mostly – and I always feel awful afterwards and wish that I hadn't done or said whatever it was that I did or said! So – next time I'm cross with you . . . if there is a next time . . . please forgive me!' Then she walked over to the hall door and, as she was going out she looked back. 'Are we friends?' she asked.

Alice nodded and smiled, but she was quite relieved when Phoebe finally went out of the room.

'Oooh!' she whispered to Spot, 'she does go on a bit. I mean, I don't see why we take so much getting used to. Mum finds us perfectly easy . . . '

'Ssssh!' Spot hissed. So, Alice, shook her head, as if trying to shake away the thoughts, and then she knelt on the floor, staring at the dog.

Spot slowly rose on to his four paws. He walked over to his water bowl and lapped some water then, tail wagging slowly, he sniffed round the bowl for any remnants of food. Having satisfied himself that he'd not left any crumbs, he sat back on his haunches and scratched behind his ear. As he did so, he, winced. Turning his head, he licked one of the scratches on his flank. Then something, perhaps a noise that Alice couldn't hear, attracted his attention. He looked towards the window. He stood up, head slightly on one side, listening. He crossed to the back door, sniffing at the crack between the door and the stone flagged floor.

'What is it?' Alice asked, rising and crossing to him.

The dog looked up at her, as she lifted the latch. Cool damp air gusted into the room. Alice shivered and reached for her anorak, from one of the pegs beside the door. She walked out into the dusk, pulling on the jacket. Spot followed her, sniffing the air and still listening intently.

An owl hooted, somewhere close at hand.

'Jasper!' Spot's voice whispered in Alice's head.

Then the sharp, surprising, bark of a fox cut through the evening from up in the trees of the valley, beyond the walled garden.

'And Cinnabar!' the voice in her head whispered again.

Alice turned and looked down at Spot. He was standing beside her, one paw raised above the ground, his head on one side, his ears pricked forward. She could feel his eager energy, as he leaned towards the sights and sounds and the smells of the forest. Her nose started to twitch as she caught the scent of the pine needles and damp earth. The owl hooted again and the fox barked. Then she noticed that other birds were singing; a loud chorus of tweeting and twittering and whistling, of long flute-like notes and short, chirpy tunes filled the distant trees with a kind of music. It was as if the whole of the forest was calling to her, pulling at her.

'Come on!' Spot said, his voice excited. And, as he spoke, Alice felt the cold through her paw as she placed it on the ground. She shook her head, sniffing the damp, scented, air again. Then, together as one, she and Spot sprang forward across the yard towards the garden gate and, pushing it open, they raced down the centre path, passing the dovecote. As they did so, Jasper, the owl, appeared from one of the topmost ledges and, swooping low, he led the way towards the forest gate. The gate was off the latch and swung backwards and forwards on the stiff breeze. Spot and Alice waited until there was a gap then pushed their way through into the dark, wind-tossed woods beyond. As they reached the forest track, Cinnabar, the fox, appeared out of the undergrowth and trotted towards them.

'Where are the others?' he asked. 'The boy never came to see me once.'

'And I have been waiting for the girl,' the owl hooted.

'Don't bother about that now,' Spot told them. 'We must find them and warn them. The badgers have been taken to Blackscar Quarry.'

The owl hooted mournfully and the red fur on Cinnabar's neck bristled.

'Blackscar!' he said.

'Cinnabar,' Spot growled, 'the boy has gone with the man to get help from the town. Wait for them on the moor road. You must lead them to Blackscar. And, Jasper, the girl is going with Meg to the badger sett. You'll find her there.'

'Where will you go, dog?' the owl hooted.

'We're going straight to Blackscar,' Spot growled.

'By which route?' Cinnabar barked.

'The fastest,' Spot replied without hesitation.

'The fastest?' Jasper hooted.

'You're going on the Dark and Dreadful path?' Cinnabar whispered.

'If we must,' Alice replied – and surprised herself with the answer.

'D'you know how awful that place is?' Cinnabar asked. 'When the hunt is out, that's where my people go to die.'

'And mine have been shot there, with slings and catapults as well as airguns and rifles,' Jasper hooted.

'It's a track made by men,' Spot said grimly, as though his words explained everything.

'But – is it the quicket way for us to get to the badgers, Spot?' Alice asked.

'The only way,' the dog whispered in her head.

'Then we have to go,' Alice said and she and Spot bounded forward without any more hesitation.

As they disappeared into the gloom of the forest, the owl sailed up above them and circled once, hooting its farewell, and the fox darted away round the side of the walled garden towards the front drive and the lane to the moor road.

'Goodbye!' Jasper called as he flew away into the night.

'Goodbye!' Cinnabar barked as he left the forest track.

'Come soon,' Spot and Alice yelped, as they started the steep ascent of the valley side.

24
The Dark and Dreadful Path

The night was dark and, although the rain had stopped, the air was still damp and cold. Thin mist wreathed the trunks of the trees and the grasses and ferns were covered with raindrops which soaked Spot's coat as they brushed past. Every one of the cuts and scratches on his body was throbbing and he was so tired that his legs trembled with every step he took.

'Please,' Alice whispered, 'we must stop.'

But Spot shook his head.

'Can't,' he gasped. 'No time.'

'Don't try to speak,' Alice whispered and then, she cried out, as a branch of bramble scraped along Spot's body and ripped at the wound on his neck.

'Oh, this is horrible, Spot,' she sobbed. 'I wish I was at home or . . . maybe we could be separate for a bit? All your body hurts so much and the pain is awful.' But, as she said the words, she felt ashamed. 'I'm sorry. That was horrid of me. If you have to suffer, then I will as well. Only I do so wish that we were both at home. I mean . . . I wish this

225

wasn't happening and that we didn't have to be here. I wish . . . '

'Don't think so much,' Spot sighed in her head. 'We must save our strength for the fight.'

'Fight?' Alice whispered, immediately afraid.

'Well, what d'you think we're going to do? Go to Blackscar and just . . . have a chat? Ask the dogs politely if they'd mind stopping killing the badgers?'

'I suppose not,' she said, feeling the fear in their body, 'I hadn't really thought what we'd do when we got there. How many dogs will there be?'

'I don't know,' Spot replied, grimly. 'Five? Ten? Maybe more. If men have come from far away, there could be a lot more than that.'

'More than ten?' Alice exclaimed. 'We can't fight ten men and their dogs, Spot. Not just the two of us.'

'And certainly not if there are any more like Fang,' Spot gasped.

'Was it Fang who did this to you?' As she spoke she gasped again as a muscle rippled at the top of a front leg, opening one of the wounds. Spot whimpered.

'Yes. It was Fang,' he replied. 'That dog and I have been waiting to have a go at each other ever since he first came to the house. When they took the badgers . . . '

'How many of them?' Alice asked. 'How many did they take?'

'Four. They left the little ones and the old sow – Betty. They took Bawson and Grey and the two sows, Trish and Stella . . . '

'Stella? She's Candy's mother,' Alice thought, remembering the little one who had come and slept on her lap. 'What happened to the others – the one that were left?'

Spot sighed.

'They were scattered. There were three dogs, last night. I fought with them all. At least it gave the little ones a chance to hide. I don't know what happened to them. I followed the men. Then Fang got my scent. His man – the builder . . .'

'Kev,' Alice prompted him.

'He . . . he set Fang on me.'

'How?' Alice asked, appalled.

'He said . . . "Go, Fang! Kill, Fang!" . . . It was like a command. That dog was like a . . . well, not like a dog. I tried to fight him . . . but I've never met such anger before.'

'Anger?' Alice whispered.

'Yes. He's been made like that. By the man, I suppose. Maybe, deep down, he's angry with him . . . Or with himself. Whatever way, when his master gives him the command to kill he has to do it. And all the time, the three men shone their torches on us and . . . laughed.' Spot sighed at the memory and his whole body shook. 'I only managed to get away because of a trick – otherwise he'd have done for me.'

'What trick?' Alice asked.

'Something the Magician taught me,' Spot replied. At the mention of the Magician, Alice's heart missed a beat.

'Oh, please, Mr Tyler – come and help us,' she cried.

'He won't. He's got his own things to do.'

'What was the trick?'

'When you're in a fight, he told me, and it's

going badly, don't resist. Do the opposite . . . give in. Go limp . . .'

'But – if you give in,' Alice protested, 'you're giving up. Then you lose.'

'No,' Spot replied, as if he also was mystified by what he was telling her, 'it works the opposite. The dog attacking you – has nothing to attack. That's when you can get away. If you're quick.'

Alice was puzzled for a moment. 'But how does it work?' she said.

'Well, think about it,' Spot said. 'If somebody was going to punch you and you went limp . . . the punch would pass right through you, wouldn't it?'

'It would still hurt you.'

'No, not really, not if you could do it properly.'

'You mean – if you ducked out of the way?'

'Yes, that's part of it. All he said was – the Magician – all he said was – "Don't resist" . . . So I didn't . . . and, for a minute, Fang had nothing to fight against and I was able to creep away. But, if his master hadn't called him off, I'd be in a bad way.'

Alice thought he seemed in a bad way even so. She could feel how the energy was sapping out of him. His pace was growing slower, his breathing heavier. He dragged his feet across the soft floor of the forest and every step he took made shafts of pain shoot through his body.

Eventually, when she thought she was going to have to force him to stop, they reached a broad track that cut across the forest in front of them.

'We're here,' he whispered and, as he did so, Alice saw the dog stagger to the centre of the path and collapse on to the ground in front of her and she realized that she was out of him once more. This sudden separation took her by surprise. She looked around in the darkness, missing the heightened awareness of Spot's dog-vision and his dog-sense, but also free of his pain and his weakness. Instead she felt her own, human, fear.

'Where are we?' she said, in a small, scared voice.

Spot didn't answer her. He was breathing heavily, gasping and groaning. Alice crossed quickly and knelt beside him, laying a hand gently on his head. Then she looked round again. The trees on either side of the track formed black, impenetrable walls; the sky above was filled with clouds, chasing across a huge silver moon. A wind was blowing that moaned and sighed. No birds sang. No animals barked or called. It was as though she and Spot were the only two living creatures in the whole of this windy, dark and forbidding world. She put her hands under her armpits and hugged herself for warmth. She felt horribly alone and afraid and then, with a sickening gasp, she understood where they were.

'This is it, isn't it?' she said. 'This is the Dark and Dreadful Path.'

Spot didn't answer. Alice leant over him, peering through the darkness at his face. His eyes were open, his breathing irregular. 'Spot,' she whispered. 'Darling Spot. What's wrong? Please tell me. What's happening?'

'The Dark and Dreadful Path,' he gasped, 'it leads . . . to . . . Death.' And he sighed, a long, trembling exhalation of breath.

* * *

Jack drove first to the police station. Bob Parker, Meg's friend, wasn't on duty but the sergeant on the desk telephoned his home and Jack was able to talk to him and to tell him what little they knew. Bob said he'd contact one or two other areas and see if any of the police had information as to where they thought the meet was going to take place.

'It's an illegal offence, you know,' Bob said, 'as well as being one of the most vile and inhuman acts. I won't tell you what I'd like to do to the so-and-so's when I catch them – because that'd be an illegal offence as well.'

'I'm going to try and find Kev,' Jack told him. 'Then we ought to meet somewhere.'

After some deliberation it was decided that they'd both phone in any information they might have gathered to the station and that they'd probably meet up later. Then Jack handed the phone back to the Duty Sergeant and Bob filled him in on what was going on, so that all the patrol cars in the area could be warned to keep their eyes open for any suspicious-looking gatherings of cars, or other clues to the whereabouts of the badger meet.

Next, Jack drove to Arthur's house, because that was the only address he had for the builders.

Arthur was having his tea and watching snooker on television.

'What's up, Mr Green?' he asked, when his wife showed Jack and William into the little kitchen, then he continued to munch slowly while Jack explained the reason for their visit.

'Yes, I dare say Kev might be involved,' he

said when Jack finished. 'He's a bit of a sports freak. He's a great supporter of Bagdale F.C.'

'This isn't sport, Arthur,' William cut in. 'It's really horrible. D'you know what they do to the badger?'

Arthur sniffed slowly and stared at William shortsightedly.

'Keen on badgers, are you?' he asked.

'Yes,' William exclaimed. Then he added, 'Well, no. I mean, I've hardly ever seen one. But I don't think it's right that men should set fierce dogs on any wild animal. I mean, that can't be right, can it?'

Arthur sniffed again and mashed potato into the gravy on his plate.

'I like the television, myself. You don't get wet, watching television. A builder doesn't like the outdoors. Too much like work.'

Eventually he revealed that Kev had recently moved to the town and that he was living in the same street as Dan.

'He'll tell you which house. I don't know. I like to keep out of things, myself. Avoid trouble, that's my line. Isn't it, Mother?' he said, staring now at his wife, who was pouring hot water into a teapot.

'We keep ourselves to ourselves,' she agreed, in a dull voice.

Impatiently Jack wrote down Dan's address and after being told the directions by Arthur, he and William hurried out of the house and back to the Land-Rover.

'How he could just sit there . . . eating . . . He

didn't *care* about the badgers . . . ' William complained.

'You'll find a lot of people are like that, Will,' Jack told him.

But Dan wasn't one of them. As soon as he heard what they had to say he ran across the street to Kev's house and banged on the door. At first there was no reply and they thought they were too late, but then a woman looked out of an upstairs window and shouted down to them to go away.

'We're looking for Kev,' Dan shouted.

'Well, you've missed him. He went out not half an hour since,' the woman replied. 'Now get off my doorstep! I'm watching telly and you're stopping me.'

'Did he say where he was going?' Jack called.

'He's walking that blessed dog up in the forest somewhere,' she shouted. 'If you see him, tell him to bring himself in some fish and chips, 'cause I've gone to bed with Frankenstein!' and with a bellow of laughter, she slammed the window shut again.

'He could be anywhere,' Jack said, gloomily.

'No. Come on,' Dan exclaimed. 'There aren't that many roads through the forest – besides, he hasn't got a car. He lost his licence, drinking and driving . . .'

'He has a friend called Ted,' William volunteered. 'At least, that's who he was with when we found him up at the sett.'

'Ted? Ted Jenkins?' Dan asked.

'I don't know,' William shrugged.

'I bet it is,' Dan said. 'He's a right little troublemaker. You know the sort: "We are the champions!" and Union Jack shorts! Well, that

232

gives us a start. Ted's got an old black van – if we look for that, we'll mebbe find them.'

'But – look where?'

'Every track in the forest, if need be,' Dan replied. 'I hate cruelty. I hate it. What did the animals ever do to the likes of Kev and Ted Jenkins? It would serve them right if the animals turned on them.'

'I can't see us covering the whole of the forest,' Jack said, glumly.

'We can get Bob Parker to look as well,' William suggested. 'We've got to do something, Uncle Jack.'

Jack returned to the police station and reported what little they'd managed to discover. Then they set out once more for the forest.

Just as Jack turned the Land-Rover on to the Moor Road, a fox jumped out in front of his headlights, making him swerve on to the verge.

'Wow! That was close!' he said. 'I never saw him coming.'

As he was still speaking, William, who was sitting next to him, opened his door and jumped out. He ran into the darkness at the side of the road.

'Cinnabar?' he called, in a whisper. 'Cinnabar!'

'Oh? You're talking to me now, are you?' a voice in his head whispered. 'I've been waiting for you to come and see me, ever since you arrived back in the valley. We knew you were here. But I gather you were so busy not believing, that you didn't even believe what you already knew you believed.'

233

'I'm sorry,' William whispered, in a contrite voice.

'Will?' Jack called, from the Land-Rover. 'Can you see anything? I didn't hit it, did I?'

'No. I don't think so,' William called. 'I'm just coming.' Then, in a whisper, he continued; 'But where, Cinnabar? Where are we to look?'

'Blackscar Quarry,' the fox replied. 'I'll be there before you are!' and, as the final words formed in William's head, the fox retraced his steps across the road, flashing red in the lights of the Land-Rover once more.

'There he is,' Dan shouted from the back seat. 'I just saw the fox again.'

'Come on, Will,' Jack called. 'We're wasting time.'

'Have you got the map, Uncle Jack?' William asked as he climbed back into the motor.

'No. You had it. Remember?' Jack replied.

'Bother,' William said. 'We've got to find Blackscar Quarry.'

'What on earth makes you say that?'

'It doesn't matter now, just help me find it.'

'I know Blackscar,' Dan said. 'I used to play there as a kid. It's a fair distance. On the other side of Goldenwater . . .'

* * *

Meg took a long time milking the cows and feeding the animals, though Mary helped as best she could. She'd have liked a milking lesson, but decided that that'd have to wait until another day. Then, when all the dogs were wolfing down bowls of food and the cats were picking at scraps, Meg collected a

234

torch and walking stick and, almost as an after-thought, her pocket camera with the flash. 'If we do happen on any lampers,' she explained, 'it frightens them a lot if they think I've got their picture – and the flash can blind them for a few seconds. You never know, it could be useful.' Then they set off at a fast pace, heading for the sett.

She didn't lead them via the bridle way that the family had taken earlier that day, but cut off through the woods, meeting the shore of the lake half way along its length. The water glimmered like steel, reflecting the moonlight through the racing clouds. The wind whipped up rows of waves that splashed against the rocks, with a sound like the sea.

'Goldenwater, it's called locally,' Meg told Mary. 'There are tales of a vast treasure hidden at its centre. I don't know so much about that – the stories of riches and treasures and great hoards of gold are longer than history in these parts – but I do know it's deep. Some even say it's bottomless. But every lake must have a bottom, mustn't it? Like every road has an end and every mountain a top. At the far end,' she pointed back along the way they were walking, and Mary saw the vague outline of a distant landscape with high cliffs and rolling mountains beyond, 'there's a waterfall. That's called Goldenspring. If you come in the summer, you'll be able to swim here – though the water is cold as ice.'

'We will be coming in the summer,' Mary told her and she looked over her shoulder again, search-ing for the waterfall in the dark recesses of the night.

As they reached the yew tree an owl hooted from its upper branches.

'Your friend again?' Meg asked, giving Mary a searching look. But she didn't wait for a reply. Her mind was on her badgers and she wouldn't pause until she had hurried down over the side of the valley to where the line of the beech trees started, sheltering the sett.

'Come on,' she called, in a high light voice. 'Come on, my babies. Come on, my dears. Betty, come on, Betty . . . ' Meg knelt on the ground calling and lightly clapping her hands together, a sound so gentle it was no louder than the beat of a bird's wings.

Mary crept stealthily down the hill, not wanting to make a sound for fear of frightening the badgers away. When she was standing immediately behind Meg, the old woman looked up at her. In the half light, Mary could see a troubled expression on her face.

'Where are they?' Meg whispered. 'Where are my little ones?' And she turned once more, calling and clapping: 'Come on! Come on, my dears! Come on, my babies!'

No badgers emerged from the trampled earth. The breeze clattered through the trees and the moonlight came and went as the clouds raced across the sky.

Jasper swayed in the branches of the yew. From his vantage-point he could see the girl and the old woman kneeling on the ground in front of her. He had been told to find them – Sirius, the dog, (or Spot as the child called him) was inclined to be bossy. 'Well,' he thought, 'I've found them. I shall now wait. The girl hasn't once tried to contact me. She seemed, actually, to expect me to come to her! She will have to be taught. I – who am as old as the night – do not . . . contact.' And he trilled his distaste so vehemently, that the sound echoed through the valley.

Cinnabar was racing up the steep side of the valley when he heard Jasper call. He stopped long enough to bark sharply in answer.

Jasper heard the call and, spreading his wings, he launched himself out of the yew and sailed over the rim of the valley, searching, with his hawk-eyes, for the tell-tale flash of Cinnabar's brush in the undergrowth below.

'I'm here,' he called.

'The boy and the man are making for Blackscar. Tell the girl. Then meet me there,' Cinnabar barked.

'Fox,' hooted the owl. 'Where are the young badgers?'

'The old sow has taken them,' Cinnabar replied, as he sprinted past.

'But taken them where?' the owl shrieked after him.

'To Blackscar,' the fox barked.

'To Blackscar?' the owl hooted mournfully. Then the girl's voice attracted his attention.

'Jasper,' Mary called. 'Oh, Jasper . . . '

'What?' the owl asked, hovering above her.

'Do you know where the badger baiting will take place?' Mary called in her mind, then, almost at once she turned and said aloud to Meg:

'Blackscar Quarry.'

'What dear?' Meg asked, looking up at her.

'That's where they've taken the badgers.'

'Then we must go at once,' Meg said, climbing up on to her feet and never once asking Mary how she knew. 'If only Mr Green has contacted Bob Parker. The police would be such a help.'

* * *

'You can't go alone,' Spot whispered.

'I can, Spot. I'll be all right. But what about you?' Alice said, trying to sound brave. But then she couldn't stop the tears from bubbling up again. 'I don't want you to die all alone here on the Dark and Dreadful Path.'

'I won't. For you I won't,' the dog gasped. 'Only . . . hurry. I'll be all right. I promise. But I shouldn't like all this to have been for nothing. Call Merula. Call him. He'll help you.'

'I don't understand,' Alice sobbed. She knew she must be brave, but she couldn't bear to see her beloved Spot so weak and ill.

'Call Merula. The Magician's blackbird . . .'

'But – it's night-time and blackbirds won't be out and besides, the Magician has given us up.'

'He'll never give you up. You're part of him,' Spot whispered. Then, filling his lungs, he howled once, a long anguished cry. 'M . . . E . . . R . . . U . . . L . . . A'.

The name echoed backwards and forwards in the close confines of the path.

'It's no use, Spot,' Alice said, sadly. 'There won't be any magic. The Magician is angry with me. I made him angry. It's my fault. So now we've got to do things on our own. Only please don't die, please, Spot. I'll do anything to stop that. I'll even go alone to the quarry. I'll tell the men the police are coming, like Meg did. Maybe that'll frighten them away – d'you think that would work?' she asked him, doubting her own words. Then, seeing the dog lying on the ground, she sobbed, 'Oh, Spot, I love you so much . . . ' and turning, determinedly, she started to walk away from him up the dark pathway.

But, after she'd taken a few steps, Alice heard above the sound of the wind and louder than the rattle of the branches, another sound. It was the eager beat of a thousand wings, accompanied by the sweet song of five hundred birds.

Alice paused and looked up. Above the tops of the trees, the clouds had cleared, revealing a nearly-full moon riding in the high sky. At once the broad path was filled with its dazzling silver light and the trees, that had seemed grim and forbidding, were transformed into enchanted boughs, tipped with sparkling light, like an avenue of Christmas trees.

'Oh, Spot, look!' Alice cried, turning round in a full circle. 'Look at the trees! It isn't such a bad place. Not when the moon is on it.' And, as she spoke, swallows darted into the clearing and swifts danced round her head. Blue tits and wagtails; thrushes and the tiny wren skimmed and chattered about her, playing and singing. Finally, dark as night herself, the Blackbird, Merula, came and alighted on Alice's outstretched hand and turned his gleaming eyes and crocus yellow beak towards her.

'Come,' he whistled, with a sound so pure and notes so rich, that Alice couldn't remember ever having heard anything so beautiful before. 'Come,' he whistled again. 'You have taken the dark away. You have given us back the silver path.'

'I have?' Alice asked, confused. 'Me? You mean me? No, I didn't do anything.'

But further protestation was useless for at that moment she was rising on the black wings of night. Up and up she flew, spiralling into the silver light, until the path below was no more than a streak on the map and the dark countryside was only relieved by the distant flashing blue light of a police car and the dull glow of lamps that illuminated the savage rent in the rock-earth that denoted Blackscar Quarry.

25
Bawson

Blackscar Quarry hadn't been worked for many years. Around its rough rock floor, bushes and thin sapling trees crowded against the sheer cliffs that enclosed it on three sides. On its fourth side two paths converged at right angles to each other. The first was an overgrown bridle way that passed between a narrow opening in the rocks and then disappeared into the murky interior of the pine forest. The other was a narrow cart track that wound steeply away from the quarry towards a distant forest road.

Usually the place was empty, visited only by the rabbits who had made it their home. In summer, the occasional walker happened on it by chance or the local youths came by once in a while to smoke cigarettes and shoot beer cans with their air pistols. It was an eerie, abandoned place, filled with shadows and the moaning wind. A ghost place, lost and forgotten.

But on this night, if any stranger had happened to pass by they would have found the customary silence disturbed by the agitated yelping of dogs and the muted voices of some twenty men, who had driven there in an assortment of cars and vans.

There was an air of intense activity and an atmosphere of excited anticipation about the place. Boxes and sacks were being unloaded from the backs of motors and the dogs strained at the thick chains and ropes by which they were tethered, smelling the strong scent of frightened badger.

At the centre of the quarry a low barricade had been constructed out of dead trunks and branches, held down with lumps of rock. It formed a rough ring which the men referred to as 'the pit'. Some of them could be seen in the light created by the headlights of their motors, positioned in a circle around the perimeter. They were all different ages from young lads to one or two grandfathers. Their eyes shone and their faces were greasy with excitement, as they trampled the ground to make it level.

Kev had tied Fang to a tree and was unloading the caged badgers, collected from the Golden Valley sett, with Ted and his friend Pete. It was Pete's first bait and he was excited and scared at the same time.

'When do we begin?' he asked Kev, as between them they lifted a cage out of the back of Ted's van.

'Soon enough,' Kev answered. 'I hope you've brought plenty of money. Fang and I feel lucky tonight.'

'That's a big 'un,' Ted said, nodding towards the cage they were carrying, 'even for your Fang. I wouldn't like to set my terrier against that one.'

'You may as well give me your money now, then,' Kev joked. 'You should get yourself a proper dog, our Ted, if you mean business. This brute'll be no match for my Fang. He could bring him down with his front paws tied together.' And he poked with a stick at the great grey badger that lay silent and panting in the cage at his feet.

'Look at the beast,' Ted said, ignoring Kev's gibes, 'you reckon we should lame it first?'

'No!' Kev exclaimed. 'Lame it? No sport in laming it. Give the dogs a bit of a run for our money. I hate an uneven battle.'

'You only say that because you've got Fang,' Ted complained, and he put his finger into the ring top of a can of lager, squirting spray as he released it.

Kev grinned and crossed over to his dog.

'I don't know why they're all afraid of you,' he said, giving Fang a flick with the end of the rope that secured him. The dog yelped with pain then growled, a deep sound.

'Oh! Temper!' Kev said, and he flicked the dog again, harder this time. 'We can't have that, can we?' and he flicked the dog once more, making it whimper, but instantly stopping the growl. 'That's better,' Kev said, 'Away you two, let's see what's to do,' and he swaggered off towards the centre of the quarry.

Left alone, Bawson, the badger, and Fang, the dog, stared at each other across the dark. The dog growled and barked, rearing up on his hind legs and straining to be free. The badger lay, snout to the ground, watching and still.

At the centre of the ring, an argument broke out between two of the men over the running order. The dogs became excited, barking and whining. Then a roar of excitement went up from the crowd. The badger looked over his shoulder. The cage he was in was only just big enough to contain him. It smelt of rabbit and had been used as a hutch. The smell filled his nostrils with fear and prison and cruelty. He could see the men gathering their dogs. The first badger was released into the pit. The dogs' barking rose to fever pitch as some of them were put into the ring.

'It's beginning,' Bawson thought and he looked back at Fang, who was straining at his leash, indignant that he hadn't yet been called.

* * *

Jack saw the blue light of the police car flickering through the dark of the forest and accelerated.

'Blackscar Quarry,' he called out of the window, as he drew level.

'Right,' said Bob Parker and he got on to the radio, calling up reinforcements. 'You follow me,' he called to Jack and, doing a sharp turn in the road, he sped away, in the lead.

* * *

When Cinnabar reached the quarry he could hear, above the din of the dogs, the sighing of the badgers. He could smell their fear. He could taste their anguish.

He skirted round, behind the line of motors, searching until he found Bawson's cage.

'Good, my fox,' Bawson whispered, greeting him.

Without hesitation, Cinnabar started to gnaw at the rope that secured the cage door. Fang barked excitedly, trying to attract Kev's attention. The fox ignored him, working frantically, but the rope was thick and Cinnabar's sharp teeth could only break through it a strand at a time.

* * *

Mary and Meg reached the rim of the quarry. Below them they could see the ring of lights and the dark shapes of the men, as they cheered and hooted their approval.

'It's begun,' Meg said, grimly.

'Come on then,' Mary said, desperately looking for a way down. But Meg put a hand on her arm.

'We can't go down, child. We'd be no match for them.'

'Then why are we here?' Mary cried.

'To be with the badgers,' Meg said, sadly. 'To watch them die.'

'No!' Mary exclaimed. 'Come on, Meg. Oh, please. We must be able to do something to stop them,' she begged.

'Well, at least we can try,' Meg said, catching Mary's urgency. 'If I could just get some photographs of the men's faces,' she continued producing a camera from her pocket and snapping up the flash, 'it would give the police something to work on. Come along, dear. There's a path down over there . . .'

* * *

Merula, the Blackbird, perched in the branch of a sapling.

'We must wait now,' he whispered.

'I can't watch,' Alice said.

'It will be all right,' a familiar voice hooted, and Jasper fluttered into the tree beside them.

245

'How do you know?' Alice cried.

'I don't,' Jasper replied. 'I'm just . . . hoping.'

* * *

'Bloody fox! Did you see that?' Kev exclaimed, kicking out at Cinnabar, who bolted into the dark as soon as the men appeared. 'He was only trying to get in the cage, wasn't he? Diabolical liberty! I hate foxes. They do a lot of damage, you know. Vermin!' he shouted, as he and Ted lifted the cage and carried Bawson to the Pit. They opened the cage door and prodded the badger out into the circle of lights. Around him a row of angry, snarling dogs gnashed and spat, straining at their collars as their masters held them back, waiting for the 'off'.

'Listen,' Bawson whispered to the dogs in each of their minds. 'Listen to me. We are all animals together. You are not my foes. We should live side by side in harmony. We are not rivals, we are not enemies. It is the men who have made you like this. Because of them, you are not . . . free. You are doing only what men have taught you. You have lost your animal-ness, you have lost your nature.'

As he spoke a little terrier snapped forward going for his front paws. Bawson backed away, batting the dog off.

'I don't want to hurt you,' he insisted. 'Why do you want to hurt me?'

'Because I hate you,' the terrier snapped.

'You don't. You don't even know me. You are only thinking thoughts you have been given. Not your own thoughts . . . the men's thoughts.'

'I don't care,' a pit bull growled. 'It's fun, killing,' and, as he barked the words, he charged forward, teeth snapping and caught Bawson a glancing blow on his cheek.

The other dogs all crowded in, snapping and barking, tearing and clawing. Bawson batted them off, using all four claws and his own teeth, but trying not to harm any of them.

'We don't have to be like this,' he pleaded with them. 'We don't have to play the human game. Your masters were once animals too. But now . . . they are beasts. We don't have to be beasts . . .'

Then, in front of Bawson the snapping, squealing crowd divided and Fang appeared. The great dog and the great badger sized each other up. A strange silence settled over the quarry.

'He's a match for him,' a man's voice rang out.

'Kill, Fang! Kill!' Kev yelled and, as he did so, he gave the dog a stinging blow with the rope across his rump, making him gasp with pain.

'D'you want to serve that man for the rest of your life, Fang?' Bawson whispered, as he braced himself for Fang's attack.

'I serve no one,' Fang growled.

'Kill, Fang! Kill!' Kev yelled again.

The dog leapt forward, sinking his teeth deep into the badger's left shoulder. The two bodies turned over, locked in a deathly embrace, their teeth snapping, their claws ripping at each other. Bawson landed on his back with Fang on top of him. With a huge surge of energy, and using all his four legs, he heaved the dog off, sending him flying through the air. Fang landed heavily on his rump but immediately got up, turning, preparing to spring again.

But, at that moment he saw the great badger, Bawson, rear up on to its hind legs. It stood, upright, blood gushing from the open wound on its shoulder, front paws jutting out, sleek head held aloft. Then, as a shaft of moonlight dazzled his eyes with its brilliance, Fang thought he saw a tall man standing where a moment before the badger had been. The man was wearing a long black coat and he carried in one hand a thin silver stick.

Fang cowered back, squealing.

'Kill, Fang! Kill!' he heard Kev yelling at him.

The dog growled, deep in his throat, trying to summon the courage to go into the attack once more.

Kev climbed into the pit, lashing the dog with his rope.

'I said kill, damn you! *Kill!*', Kev yelled, his fury overwhelming him, thrashing the dog viciously as he spoke.

Fang leapt forward, the lashing from Kev still stinging on his back. As the man held aloft his silver stick, Fang jumped for his arm, and sank his teeth deep into muscle above the wrist.

'Is this the only language you know, poor Fang?' he heard a quiet voice whisper in his ear. 'Then, kill Fang, kill!'

Fang squealed once, dropping to the ground. Then he turned and faced Kev across the pit.

'Damn you, I said kill, Fang!' Kev snarled at him.

Fang sprang across the ring straight at Kev, with all his pent-up anger and hatred seething out of him in a ferocious, blood-chilling, roar.

'Watch out, he's gone amok!' Ted yelled.

Kev raised his arm, fending off the powerful dog as best he could. The other dogs started to bark and snap. Some turned on each other and one or two them even attacked their masters as well.

'What the hell is going on here?' one of the men yelled. His mates were already running for the safety of their motors.

But now, suddenly, the air around them was filled with birds. Their wings beating, they flew round the men, skimming down on to them and away from them, like a swarm of bees. The men had to duck and dodge, flailing out with their arms. The badgers in the sacks were clawing their way free. A fox leapt out of the dark and sank his teeth into Pete's ankle. An owl dropped from the sky and sank its claws into Ted's neck. He brushed it off with a shout.

'What the hell's happening?' he cried.

At the same moment a little old lady appeared in front of him and a camera flashlight sparked in the dark. Before he could even comprehend what had taken place, Meg had dodged away as she went from man to man, taking as many pictures as she could.

Mary meanwhile was releasing the badgers from their cages and sacks, tearing at the fastenings with her fingers. As each badger was freed, it turned and, instead of running for cover, it entered the fray, joining the dogs and the birds in the assault on the men.

Alice appeared, as if from nowhere. She ran straight to where Bawson was lying on the ground, blood oozing from his shoulder.

'Oh, Mr Tyler,' she whispered as she dabbed

at the badger's wounds with her handkerchief, 'I'm so sorry.'

Kev had managed to kick himself free of Fang. He ran, limping, towards Ted's van. Ted reached the van at almost the same moment.

'Let's get the hell out of here,' Kev gasped. But Fang leapt at him again from behind, pulling him down on the ground.

'Help me, Ted,' Kev yelled, reaching out a hand as he fell.

'Not likely,' Ted replied, scrambling into the van. 'You're on your own, mate.'

The sound of motors being started cut through the pandemonium. Men were shouting to each other. The dogs were barking and squealing.

Just as the first car was reversing to turn, a police car slid into the quarry, blocking the exit, its blue light flashing. It was followed by Jack's Land-Rover, which squealed to a halt. Jack and William and Dan leapt out, surveying the scene in front of them with disbelief.

Distantly, the sound of police sirens heralded the arrival of reinforcements.

'Run for it, lads!' one of the men yelled, turning, and starting a mass rush towards the only other exit: the Dark and Dreadful Path. But as they reached the gap in the rocks, they found their way barred by a bedraggled but vicious black and white dog.

'Spot!' Alice yelled, pushing through the crowd and standing beside him. Then she also turned and faced the men.

'You all stay where you are,' she sobbed, the tears – of relief as well as of anger and misery –

welling out of her eyes. 'You stay where you are. You . . . revolting, vile, cruel people.'

'Get out of the way,' a man shouted, as he pushed past her, knocking her to the ground.

Alice fell to her knees, sobbing. All around her was chaos as the men tried to escape. But the opening was narrow and gradually they gave themselves up. Some hung their heads. The sight of the small girl, kneeling sobbing in front of them tugged at their sentimental hearts.

'Don't cry, lass,' one of the older men said. 'It was just a bit of fun we were having.'

'Fun?' Alice yelled and she threw herself at the man, pummelling him with her fists, as though she wanted to destroy him.

'Hey! You little vixen,' the man exclaimed. 'I'll have you up for assault and battery. You can't treat me like that,' and he gripped Alice in his strong arms.

'Put her down,' a grim voice behind him ordered.

The man turned in time to see Jack's fist, going straight for his chin.

'Oh, Uncle Jack!' Alice exclaimed, brimming with pride as she picked herself up off the ground. 'I think you've knocked him out!'

26
A Fair Wind and a Full Moon

They all slept late at Golden House the following morning and the sun was high in the sky by the time breakfast was served in the kitchen.

Phoebe had been too concerned about their welfare to be cross and even Alice escaped with no more than a reprimand.

'You can't go rushing off in the middle of the night all on your own, Alice. What would your mother and father think of us?' she said.

'I'm sorry,' Alice told her. 'But I wasn't really alone, Phoebe. I was with Spot. And Mum and Dad would understand, I'm sure they would.'

Jack and Dan had carried Bawson back to the Land-Rover. Then they drove to Four Fields with Meg. They took Spot with them. Meg said she would be getting the vet first thing the following morning to look at Bawson and she thought it would be as well if he saw the dog as well.

The other badgers had slipped away into the night. The Golden Valley sett hadn't far to go. They'd found Betty and the young cubs, huddled under a tree at the top of the quarry cliffs, where they had watched the ghastly spectacle, unable to move for fear, and had been reunited with Grey and Stella and Trish, who had mercifully survived the dogs.

Meg, meanwhile, had been fretting about what would happen to the badgers that had been brought by baiters from outside the area.

'Perhaps they'll make new homes here,' she'd said, 'but I doubt it. They'll pine for their own families, you see. That's why Betty wouldn't stay away. The family means everything to a badger. I fear they'll try to get home and that could mean crossing miles of unknown country.'

The police had rounded up all the badger baiters and taken their details. One or two of the rowdiest had been put under arrest. The dogs had taken some quietening down, particularly Fang, who'd had to be stunned before anyone could handle him. An ambulance had come to take Kev to hospital. As for the birds, they'd simply disappeared back into the dark trees and blended with the night. In time they became no more than a vague memory, the stuff of legends, to be added to the other magic tales of Golden Valley.

'I've never seen birds behaving like that before,' Bob Parker had repeated more than once. 'Out in the middle of the night? Mobbing humans? What on earth was going on?'

'They were helping their friends,' Meg had said quietly, and she had looked at the children as she spoke, as if suggesting that perhaps she meant them.

Eventually Bob had driven the children home to Golden House in his panda car. They'd found Phoebe pacing up and down on the drive, anxiously scanning the trees for sign of them and she'd been so relieved to see them safe that she'd hugged them all to her and cried and wasn't cross once.

Now, with the light, some of the horrors of the previous night began to ease away. They had arranged to go and see Meg at Four Fields, but it was decided that they would wait until after lunch, to give the vet plenty of time to make his visit.

The children waited until the coast was clear and then they hurried up the steps to the secret room. To their surprise, the Magician was waiting for them. He looked older and sadder and the arm that usually held the silver stick was in a thick white sling.

As soon as Alice saw him, she ran across the room and threw her arms round him. The force of her weight made him wince, but he put his good arm round her waist and hugged her close.

'Well done, Alice,' he said. Then, looking over her shoulder at the other two, he smiled and nodded. 'And well done all of you.'

'Oh, Mr Tyler, I thought I'd never see you again,' Alice said. 'And the thought was so dreadful that I . . . I couldn't bear it.'

'You had to think that, Alice,' he told her, gently. 'You had to act from your own conviction. You had to act with your own courage. The danger of magic is that you can come to rely upon it. You expect it to do things for you. It is all very well being brave but, if you secretly know that at the wave of a wand you can change the order of things, then it does rather spoil the valour, doesn't it? But you had to be brave all on your own. And you were. You were brave and fierce and strong. You acted from your heart and your only weapon was love. I'm so proud of you, Alice. You are a true Constant and you will be constantly true. You will ever be my companion in this work. I told you all that you had to come to understand the natural world. It is a simple world that has been muddled and muddied by the deeds of Men. But it is not too late for our world. It will be, I think, never quite too late so long as people learn to act from the heart, and not from greed for riches or lust for power. Only the heart can save the natural world, for it is the heart that is in tune with nature. That is where the under-standing lies. It is from the heart that you respond to the beauty of a sunset or the wonder of a rose. It is the heart that hears the blackbird's song, it is the heart that smells the wild honeysuckle. It is the heart that allows you to enter into the Dog, Sirius, and the Fox, Cinnabar, and the Owl, Jasper. It is the heart that hears and feels and smells and tastes and sees all the wonders of this world. You three have good hearts. You three Constant children. My companions. My friends.'

He paused and there was silence in the room. Alice didn't look at William and Mary. She was too embarrassed. She thought that the Magician's long speech had been a bit over the top really. She hadn't been all that brave, in fact most of the time she'd been so scared that she could hardly breathe. And anyway it had been Spot that had done most of the brave things. But it was nice to be specially praised and she was so glad to see the Magician again that she decided not to say anything. But then she remembered something that she did just want to say, though it was almost more to William and Mary than to Stephen Tyler.

'The Dark and Dreadful Path isn't really all that bad, you know. So I wasn't being very brave. The moon came out and all the trees looked like Christmas trees and it was so light that it wasn't ghostly at all.'

Stephen Tyler cried out delightedly.

'The Silver Path!' he exclaimed. 'Oh, that is good news! You see, this place, this Golden Valley, is particularly special because it is a place where three great energy lines – you know what these are?' The children shook their heads. 'No, well you will one day. They are the ancient paths, that our fore-fathers understood and used. They are the sacred paths, where the energies of the earth are at their most potent. Here in Golden Valley we have two paths close together. The Golden path and the Silver path and between them, entirely because of them, there is a third, hidden, quite unique and secret path. It has no name and, in some ways, it is still unexplored. But the Silver path lost its power. Men cut down the beech woods and planted foreign pines. The animals left it, birds wouldn't fly there, even the moon could not penetrate through the thick branches. When the power went from the Silver path, the balance went with it. That is why this house was falling into ruin. That is why Jonas Lewis was so easily corrupted. A corruption at Golden House? It cannot be possible. That is why, eventually, the emblem was removed.'

Stephen Tyler sighed, remembering only the sad thoughts. Alice yawned. He was talking a bit above her head again and Mary shuffled her feet

256

and wondered if it was going to be a long lecture. She had heard a car arriving down on the drive and was wondering who it might be who had come to call.

But William, however, was eagerly listening to the old man's words and now excitedly exclaimed;

'Yes, yes. That's what I think I saw when we were flying in the Kestrel. The country below us reminded me of the picture I saw on the chimney breast when I found the steps up the chimney. And the pendant that Jack found and gave to Phoebe. It's all the same, isn't it? And the weather vane. I'm right, aren't I?'

Stephen Tyler looked at him deeply.

'Your time is coming, William Constant. That brain must be opened. When will you next be here for a considerable time?'

'The summer holidays,' William replied.

'We'll have high jinks in the summer holidays,' the Magician told him.

'What? Just William?' Alice protested.

'Certainly not. All of you.'

'Where did the weather vane come from?' Mary asked.

'The top of the dovecote,' Stephen Tyler replied. 'Now it could be replaced. It would be a good time. For tonight we will have a fair breeze and a full moon.'

He sighed again, as if he was in pain, and lifted his arm into a more comfortable position in the sling.

'Is your arm very bad?' Alice asked him.

'Of course it's bad,' he replied irritably. Then he smiled, apologetically. 'You remember – a dog bit it. I must go. Perhaps tonight we might be together at the tree house. You have yet to see it with the lantern alight. But only if it is convenient. You have done enough, you three. You have given us back the Silver path.'

And he left them in the secret room, fading into his own time, with a long, weary sigh.

When they returned to the hall they discovered that Dan had come to see them. He was still full of all that had happened at Blackscar Quarry the night before and he was anxious to reassure them that Arthur and he wanted to continue working on the house if they were still welcome.

'Of course you are,' Phoebe told him, as she gave him a second helping of cherry cake. 'It isn't your fault that Kev turned out to be so horrid.'

'I don't think he'll ever do it again, though,' Dan said. 'I should think what happened last night will stay with him for the rest of his life.'

'What will happen to Fang?' Alice asked.

'He's got the be put down, I'm afraid. That dog's completely out of control. A real vicious brute.'

'Poor Fang,' Alice said.

'Oh, no!' Mary groaned. 'She's not going to start being sorry for Fang now, is she?'

'I can't help it if I have a big heart,' Alice said with a superior shrug, then she burst out giggling and made the others laugh as well.

As Dan was leaving, William caught him up and they had a moment's whispered conversation before they both disappeared together round the back of the house.

'What's William up to?' Alice asked.

'I don't know,' Mary said, sounding preoccupied. Then she ran a hand through her hair. 'I think I'll wash my hair,' she said.

'Mary?' Alice said, looking at her suspiciously. 'What are you up to, for that matter?'

'Nothing,' Mary replied, innocently.

'You've got that funny look. . . . Oh, no!' she sighed, suddenly realizing. 'You're falling in love with Dan now. Oh, fishcakes!'

'No, I am not,' Mary protested, crossly. And she ran into the house, confirming Alice's suspicions.

They returned to Four Fields that afternoon, driving there in the Land-Rover. Meg welcomed them on the doorstep and Spot appeared, with a bandage round one shoulder and looking very sorry for himself. But he did manage to wag his tail when he saw Alice.

Meg gave them tea and sausage rolls that she'd bought specially off the travelling shop that visited her once a week. Alice had never tasted anything so delicious since she didn't know when, but she didn't say so for fear of upsetting Phoebe.

They stayed until dusk, then Phoebe and Jack drove home with Stephanie, and the children walked back through the woods to the yew tree with Meg. She wanted to see that Bawson had got home safely and that the other badgers were all settling back in at the sett. The vet had given Bawson an antibiotic injection but apart from that they had decided to let nature be the healer. The big badger had been impatient to get back to his family and as soon as he was able to move he had lumbered off across the meadow and disappeared from sight.

A stiff breeze was blowing when they reached the edge of the valley. The light was fading from the sky and, as they watched, a perfect silver disc of a moon rose out of the ragged trees on the horizon.

The children climbed the yew to the secret house and Meg went down the hill to be with her badgers.

William had brought a box of matches and with one he lit the candle that was stuck into the sconce inside the old lantern. Then, one by one, they opened all the shutters of the pointed windows. The air swirled in about them, fresh and cold. The lantern swung from side to side, casting pale shadows. Then, as the moon rose in the sky and grew stronger, a tiny circular disc appeared deep down in the valley, where the chimneys of the house could just be seen. It glittered and shone with the intensity of a searchlight, a mirror-image of the moon itself.

'It's the window of the secret room,' William said, thinking aloud. 'Those metal mirrors behind the candles sconces. That's what they're for. To reflect the moon and to reflect the sun. And look!'

In between the house and the steep side of the valley tiny lights were flashing.

'What is it?' Alice asked.

'It's the weather vane. Dan helped me put it up. You remember how there were four little discs on that metal cross that went below the sun and the moon? I think what happens is, the wind blows them round and they reflect the light.'

'But, what are they for?' Mary asked, puzzled.

'Fun.' a voice behind them replied and turning they saw Stephen Tyler come into the room. 'Why must everything be for something? They are a beacon. They are a light to guide us. But most of all . . . they are fun. Oh, see how the valley sparkles! And listen . . . '

The owls were hunting in the night and somewhere a fox barked.

'Breathe,' the old man said.

The air was heavy with the perfume of pine and honeysuckle, of rich damp earth and of the fresh dew.

'This is the world of nature,' the old man whispered. 'The moon is reflecting the sun. The balance is perfect. Out there is life and death, the badger and the fox are going about their business. All's well.'

'D'you remember,' Alice said, 'how we found the door in the tree? I've always thought there'd be a door in a tree. It seemed right somehow. But . . . I never really believed I'd find one. Did you, Mare?'

But Mary didn't answer. She didn't want to lose the sounds of the night. And William . . . he was trying to work out how it had all happened.

Alice sighed contentedly to herself. The badgers were safe, Spot hadn't died on the Dark and Dreadful Path and most of all, the magician had forgiven her.

'Next time we come we'll have ages here,' she thought.

The Tunnel Behind the Waterfall

Book III of The Magician's House

' . . . 'William felt a huge surge of energy. It was as though he'd reached out and taken hold of a swiftly moving vehicle and now, having been whipped off his feet, he was being dragged along at an alarming speed.

'Here we go!' the otter-voice in his head whispered and then with a piercing 'Aaaahhhh!' of desperate sound, which William suspected was more of his making than the otter's, they both, as one, hurtled towards the narrow opening.

We'll never make it!' William screamed, mentally ducking his head and trying to avoid the hard, jagged rocks that sped towards them.

The sound of the water roared in his ears. The rocks closed in tighter and tighter all around his otter-body. They turned and dodged and flicked and spiralled down and through the solid earth.

'Blackwater Sluice!' a voice screamed in his head . . .'

It is the long summer holiday and William, Mary and Alice are immediately plunged into another desperate adventure as they fight to save the Golden Valley from the greedy schemes of the developers who are doing the work of the Magician's evil assistant, Matthew Morden. It is a crusade that will take the children deep below Golden Valley and into The Place of Dreams; the battle over Goldenwater has to be fought and the terrible Crow to be conquered, as, little by little, they draw closer to time travelling.

THE TUNNEL BEHIND THE WATERFALL is available in Red Fox paperback, price £3.99.

ANN COBURN

*B*e warned: where the edges of past and present merge and the borders of time blur... expect the unexpected.

Four very different buddies: Alice, Frankie, David and Michael, have one thing in common - photography. But their passion for cameras is developing into a very dangerous hobby...

1 WORM SONGS   ISBN 0 09 964311 1   £3.99

2 WEB WEAVER   ISBN 0 09 964321 9   £3.99

3 *And coming soon!*
DARK WATER   ISBN 0 09 964331 6   £3.99

THE BORDERLANDS SEQUENCE by Ann Coburn
Out now in paperback from Red Fox